(Cover and interior art by Sandy Peraza)

To Tucker, as much joy reading I wish you as I had writing!.

Derek Rey

Asher's Garden

By Derek Rey Pangelinan

Derek Rey Pangelinan
Portland, Oregon

ISBN 978-1-7359265-0-6

First Edition, December 2020

Contents

Prologue

The sun spilled into Asher's living room from wide windows and fell warmly on his cheek. That same light gently blanketed Mrs. N. who sat sleeping on the nearby couch. He was reading a book given to him by his mother; the book was about gardening on a patio. A patio was about all that the Jakes family had to work with, so they had recently begun their garden on the deck of their second-floor apartment. Asher's favorite thing to do was read. He probably enjoyed reading about gardening more than the actual gardening itself. He was in the middle of a section describing some efficient methods of nurturing tomato plants in small spaces when he heard several voices yell in unison outside his home, followed by tires squealing and the loud thud of a blunted impact. He bolted to the sliding-glass door and ripped it open to make his way to the railing of the deck that held their new garden to see what kind of wreckage lay down in the street in front of his home. Asher saw several people he knew down on the street level. Mr. Harper, J.J. and K.K., a local homeless gentleman who was missing a leg, were all gazing toward the nearby intersection. He looked in that direction and when he saw… he fell backward, his eyes rolled back into his head, and he was unconscious.

The newscaster fixed her gaze on the teleprompter; a breaking story was coming, and it was her job to deliver it. A producer handed her a sheet with the newly inked story—not knowing what she was about to say, she read with confidence and determination like she was trained to do:

"We have a breaking story. Just down 2 blocks from our KCMW station near the corner of S.W. Clay and S.W. Park; our news crew is the first on the scene of a one-vehicle accident. Multnomah County Fire and Rescue workers are attending to Lynn Jakes, the well-known, weekly columnist for the Oregonian, and her son Simon. No, I'm sorry... my producers are informing me that Lynn Jakes has already been pronounced dead, but her son is alive—although in critical condition. Our cameras are showing that Simon is being placed onto a stretcher and loaded into a late-arriving ambulance on the way to St. Vincent's Medical Center. Matthew Maxwell, our location-reporter has been able to gather some information. Tell us Matthew, have you learned any additional details about this tragedy? What caused it? Can you tell us about Lynn Jakes?"

"Thanks Jenny. And yes, I have learned a bit from some bystanders here. Apparently, there was a small animal that ran in front of the vehicle, causing Lynn Jakes to swerve and fall into a recently dug hole about 20 feet wide and only 7 feet deep; it's the beginning of a project that local utility workers started today. Medics here say the impact of hitting the wall of the hole must be what caused the injuries and death. And very sadly, Lynn Jakes' destination was only about 50 feet away; some of the bystanders here are her neighbors and tell me that she lived in the apartment that

*you see behind and above me with her two sons, Simon and
Asher, and her husband Ray. I have nothing more at this
moment, the utility crew is gone for the day and no one is
willing to speak on camera, honestly all here seem to be
paralyzed by grief and shock. Matthew Maxwell, KCMW
News. Back to you, Jenny."*

*"Thank you, Matthew. We'll continue to report on this
as information comes in on the condition of Simon Jakes,
the son of the columnist for the Oregonian, Lynn Jakes.
Lynn was well known for her volunteer work supporting the
Washington Park Zoo and other wildlife charities. We'll
take a short break now but when we come back, we'll hear
from Ron Bernard on how the Ducks and Beavers are
faring in their fall football camps."*

As the lights above the cameras turned off, Jenny Neighbors
watched producers put together a graphic of Lynn Jakes' picture
from stock photos and the dates 1950-1985. Curly blonde hair,
blue eyes, and slightly crooked white teeth filled the monitor and
stared back at Jenny as a tear pooled in the corner of her left eye.
She held back the need to cry and resolved that a good journalist
must separate herself from a story to deliver the truth—even if
you're faced with the fact that one of your closest friends has just
died. She will let herself grieve when she gets home tonight.

In another world, not so very far away, a ladybug and two
spiders were tending a garden. Bugs with hoes and shovels would
be a rather peculiar sight to most, but to the creatures here, it was
just as things were. They enjoyed the work together—as good

friends always do—and they'd tell you about the history of their heart-felt friendships, but they had no memory of any. They might even tell you about their families and childhood memories if they had any, but they didn't. They would tell you how they came to know the matriarchal moth that sat nearby on a stump or the bespectacled, five-legged ant crawling toward the garden, but they can't seem to recall any such moments. You could ask about the vegetables and herbs and roots they grew and the love they felt for their friends and neighbors and get wonderfully detailed answers with unmistakable sincerity, but don't ask about yesterday, they simply didn't know there even was a yesterday.

Day 1 – A Boy and His Garden

The Rocks in the Park Blocks

Asher sat at his desk in Mrs. Good's 6th grade classroom. He and his best friend, Lucie, were looking at her freshly scraped knee, studying the tiny pearls of blood as they grew and formed solid lines of red. She nearly stained her shirt leaning in to get a closer look. Asher marveled at her ability to take pain. They were waiting for Asher's father, Ray, to pick them up from school so they could all walk home together; it was just a block and a half through the Park Blocks, and it was tradition.

"Hey, I've got a plan," Asher said as he focused his mischievous blue eyes on Lucie.

Lucie knew that Asher's "plans" (as he called them) were always fun and usually resulted in laughs or sweet edibles or spare change from his father's pocket—three of the most important things to a couple of twelve-year-olds.

"Okay, whatcha got?" Her shoulder length brown hair bobbed as she turned her ear toward Asher, so he could remain quiet.

"Well, when my dad gets here, hide your scraped knee under your pant-leg. When we walk into the park and you see the rocks, climb up with me and then we'll pretend to bump into each other. Then you can fall off and pretend to hit your knee. When my dad looks at it, he'll want to make you feel better so he'll get us some ice cream at Bruno's."

"Good plan! Except it's called gelato." Lucie stuck her tongue out at Asher and he quickly pinched it.

"You're never going to learn, are you?" Asher shook his condescendingly.

"Your fingers taste like dirt!" Lucie spat as she made an 'eewww gross' face.

"I'm a kid who plays in the dirt, DUH!" Asher wiped his guilty thumb and finger on his orange t-shirt. "Pull your pant-leg down, it's 2:29." Asher's father used to be late all the time, but since Asher's mother died late last summer, he had been right on time every day, even early. Asher noticed the difference but just attributed it to one of the many ways that his father had become more attentive to the needs of their now-smaller family, most notably the quantity and quality of hugs.

The bell rang. Mrs. Good opened the door and there stood all the parents waiting for their children. Among them was Asher's dad, Ray, average height and thin in a plain blue t-shirt, zip-up sweatshirt, jeans, and brown leather hiking boots looking the perfect part of the Portlander that he was: comfortable, casual, and active. More importantly, he blended into the background of the visual noise of Portland, unnoticeable in every way and that's exactly what he wanted.

The open and sunny Park Blocks were a green, bright backdrop to the waiting parents. Ray came into the classroom and gave Asher a dependable hug and asked him and Lucie to collect their things as he walked up to the teacher. "Hi, Mrs. Good." Ray reclusively stuck his hands in the pockets of his well-worn jeans. "Is there anything you want Asher to work on this summer before he starts the seventh grade?"

"Hello Mr. Jakes, thank you for asking." She feigned concern. "He really should work on his academics; straight A's just won't do in the seventh grade." Margery Good was a fine teacher and knew how to communicate what needed to be heard. That's why Ray and Lynn had chosen St. Andrew's Primary; it had a reputation for caring, excellent teachers. "If there was anything, I guess you could find some kind of summer camp or program that would introduce him to something new. It could be anything really, just as long as it's new to him. That would probably be healthy for his mind."

Ray thought about what Mrs. Good had suggested. "Something new? That might be hard; he can be picky. I don't know if he'll enjoy something new right now."

"He will if you let him lead you Mr. Jakes. He'll tell you when he's really interested in something. Just start making suggestions."

"Yeah, that makes sense." Ray nodded in agreement. His brow furrowed and he turned his eyes slightly away, "and anyway, it'll be good to keep him busy."

"Yes…" said Mrs. Good, concern crawling across her face. She knew that Ray was worried about Asher's idle thoughts of losing his mother only a year ago. Not only were their lives turned inside out, upside down, and backwards by the loss of Asher's mother, but his brother Simon never did wake from the coma that took him immediately after the accident. Ray still visits Simon daily and Asher usually visits their next-door neighbor during that time.

Ray turned and looked at the two children. "Alright kids, say 'goodbye' to the sixth grade and 'hello' to the summer of 1986!!" Ray's attempt at enthusiasm was wildly overshadowed by his discomfort brought on by that very attempt.

Lucie humored him, her voice splitting the air, a thin, bright bell across an open field, "Goodbye sixth grade, HELLOOOO summer!"

Toting backpacks and lunchboxes, they walked out of the classroom and into the bright, mid-afternoon sun of late spring in Portland. Ray held Asher's and Lucie's hands as they looked both ways, crossed the street, and entered the shaded grass of the Park Blocks. They thought they were too old for the hand-holding; Ray wouldn't even entertain the idea of not holding their hands while crossing a street.

Some have tried to compare Portland's Park Blocks with Central Park or The Mall in Washington D.C., citing its picturesque landscaping with towering trees that create a shading canopy fifty to a hundred feet up. They point out the historic architecture of the neighboring buildings and the park's central placement within an arts and education district; Portland State University claims six of the twelve blocks while two art museums and two concert halls and various historic locales of Portland surround the other six blocks.

Truth be told, the Park Blocks were nothing like Central Park or The Mall. It does have about a dozen or so points of interest and the trees are beautiful, but there is no Shakespeare in the Park. There are no trails or mirror pond and no Washington Monument nearby, although there is a rather large sculpture of Teddy Roosevelt on a powerful-looking horse with some inscription of "The Rough Riders…" on a plaque—apparently a donation by a doctor who claimed to have treated the president and retained his friendship. It's simply twelve blocks of city park all in a neat row, not even the average size of your normal city block; it's a little narrow in one direction so when viewed on a map, it appears as a long and very thin green rectangle. Asher considers it a part of his home. He lives in a second-floor apartment in a building owned by Lucie's parents, just on the east side of the Park Blocks, a block and a half south from his school and a block and a half north from Portland State University. Asher and Lucie have lived around the corner from each other their entire lives and the Park Blocks have been their playground.

In the center of the park block directly across from St. Andrew's Elementary School is Peace Chant, a work of modern art that's a collection of three massive granite stones, each about twelve to fifteen feet in length and four feet wide with two laying on their sides and one standing high, dominating the space. These are what Asher and Lucie call "the rocks."

The three of them stopped at the rocks. It was a daily ritual; lying backpacks and lunchboxes down, Asher and Lucie began an adventure. Lucie took charge and jumped onto one of the rocks, raised an imaginary sword in the direction of the vertical rock, and yelled, "You will not take our castle!!" Seeing his son like this was one of the few things that Ray looked forward to these days. He turned and looked toward the corner of S.W. Park and S.W Clay and felt a tension well up inside. A scream and a rustling pulled him out of a painful memory as he quickly turned to see Lucie on the ground holding her knee.

"Oh sweetie, let me take a look. Are you okay?" She pulled up her pant leg to reveal a patch of bloody skin. Ray pulled a tissue from the travel-pack of tissues he carried during allergy season and dabbed at her knee. Ray saw that she was clearly trying to be strong and hold back tears; Asher saw that she was clearly a magnificent actress and gave her the thumbs-up.

"There, the bleeding stopped." Ray was glad to help Lucie. "I've got an idea. Why don't I take you two to Bruno's? It'll be a nice way to celebrate the end of another school year."

"YESSS!" Lucie shrieked as only Lucie could. "Thank you, Mr. Jakes."

Asher jumped up and yelled, "Yeah, ice cream—er, I mean—gelato!"

Ray laughed at his son as he helped Lucie up and they began the short trek to Bruno's, just on the opposite side of the building on the same city block on which Asher and Ray lived. Asher and Lucie stole a glance at each other and knew that they just chalked up another victory.

A Cherimoya and the
Adult Conversation

A little while later, Ray and the two children were walking out of Bruno's, each with a cone of gelato. Asher and Lucie each got chocolate and Ray had tiramisu, a favorite of his since a trip to Italy many years ago. They turned left, then another left at the end of the block, walked a short distance and were in front of Lucie's parents' produce market all very quietly, mouths filled with gelato. Asher and Lucie loved that so many great places were all on the same city block – his home on the park side to the west, Bruno's on the east side, Lucie's parents' produce market and home on the north side and JJ's Diner - where Asher and Ray eat most of their meals - was in the southwest corner, on the bottom floor of Asher's apartment building. Ray explained to Asher once that "that's just how cities are made." Lucie's parents owned everything on the block except for the space that JJ's occupied and knew that in cities, having everything in walking distance is a good thing; for Lucie Harper and her parents, it was ideal that home and work shared a wall and a door.

Harper's Produce Market was a large, open-air space with a green, translucent corrugated roof. Dozens of produce-filled tables were lined up side-by-side and end-to-end making meandering paths throughout the market guiding customers along to see myriad fruits, vegetables, and herbs, both exotic and common to the Portland neighborhoods. Sprays hung over each table and misted the stock at regular intervals.

Asher, Lucie, and Ray entered the market between the dark purple eggplant and a table with six hot-house tomato varieties including two yellow ones that always caught customers' eyes. Lucie immediately ran to her father who was pulling damaged onions off of a table and was tossing them into a box on the bottom of a three-tiered cart.

"Hi Sweets!" Frank Harper held his arms open and scooped up his daughter. Mr. Harper was a short, burly man with huge forearms and calloused hands with bratwurst-thick fingers from years of hard work. When Lucie was a toddler and first saw a gorilla in a television show, she thought that it looked like her father in stature. Lucie burrowed into her father's gorilla chest, and the crinkle of his green, plastic apron between them sounded like love and protection to her.

Frank put her down and reached for a heart-shaped, soft-ball-sized, dark-green fruit that was soft to the touch. He handed it to Lucie then sat her on the top of the cart and explained to his daughter, "It's a cherimoya. Split it open with your fingers like this and then eat the white part around the seeds. Don't swallow the seeds, you might grow a cherimoya tree in your stomach." Lucie's faced scrunched in annoyance at her father; but it melted back to curiosity as she broke into the fruit. Frank called, "Asher, come and try this, you two tell me what you think of it."

"That's nice of you Frank," Ray said appreciatively.

Frank pulled Ray a few tables down from the two children at the cart studying the new fruit, miniature judges at some exotic food show. Frank's face betrayed him with unmistakable anxiety. "Ray, we need to talk. I don't know how to say this easily, so I'll just say it straight. You've been a good tenant of mine for... what, almost fifteen years now? I consider you a friend, so I think I owe it to you to tell you that Anne and I might be selling all of our property on the block." Ray stopped eating his gelato. He was shocked but stayed quiet and listened as Frank went on. "Out of nowhere we got an amazing offer. The places weren't even on the market."

"Does Mrs. Neighbors know?" Alta Neighbors had lived in her apartment alone for almost thirty-five years, right across the hall from the apartment that Ray and Asher, and at one time, the entire Jakes family lived.

Frank nodded, "She knows—I've spoken to her. I'll come up tomorrow morning and we'll talk more." Frank had customers waiting and some information to gather from the children about the cherimoya. Frank and Ray walked back over to the children.

"Dad, I love it!" Lucie said, now with a little bit of the white cherimoya flesh mixed with the chocolate at the corner of her mouth.

Asher jumped in, "It's kind of messy, Mr. Harper, but it's really sweet, I like it."

"Okay then, I'll put it next to the pineapples. Next time you two have one, go over to the park and you could have a seed-spitting contest. I tell you, God created cherimoyas just for the seed-spitting; they're the best."

Frank picked Lucie up off of the cart and as he set her down, his eyes were level with the onion table he had been working with and he spotted a very obviously damaged onion. "Hey! I thought I finished this table." He saw several more damaged onions on the table. "I must be losing my good eyes." He began to pull a few and saw a spot of chocolate gelato on one. "Lucie!"

"I didn't do it Dad, Asher did!"

"No, I didn't!"

"You two be quiet, I know you better than that. Whoever did it, the other thought it was a good idea. Now get out of here before I make you sweep the floor."

The two schemers stood with guilty grins and not-sorry eyes and steeled all their will to hold their composure.

"Say 'goodbye' Lucie and go wash up. Help your mother get dinner ready, she's cooking spaghetti and she says she wants to teach you how to make the sauce today."

They all said their goodbyes and Ray and Frank looked at each other, a knowing glance that tomorrow would bring a sobering conversation.

Frank turned to the table, Lucie skipped along to the back of the market where a door led to the Harper's home, and Ray and Asher left the market.

Gotta Save a Worm's Life

After leaving Harper's, Asher and Ray went home which was just a short walk around the corner. The deck to their apartment provided the eve to a small sundries store beneath and some leaves and vines could be seen poking through the black wrought iron railing of the deck. The two of them would have continued a few more steps to the door to take stairs up to their apartment, but Asher abruptly stopped and held his father's arm, stopping him from taking another step. Ray looked down at his son, who seemed to be focused on something on the sidewalk in front of them.

"Dad, I think that's an earthworm."

"Well, it rained this morning. It probably came out of the ground to keep from drowning in the saturated dirt."

"But it stopped raining before recess today. Recess is at 9:10 so why didn't it go back underground? It's the only one."

Ray is always patient with Asher's curiosities; it comes with the territory of being the father of an active and growing mind. "It probably got too far away from the dirt and got too dry when the sun came out. When an earthworm gets too dry, it doesn't move as well and then usually just dies. They don't drink water like most animals, they soak it in through their skin."

"I know that Dad, it's called osmosis."

Ray laughed. "Yup. That it is, son."

Asher bent down and picked up the worm and looked closely at it, feeling the leathery skin, not seeing any eyes but only a tiny hole that Asher knew to be a mouth.   Ray said to his son, "Did you know that earthworms have seven hearts?"

"No, they don't. They have five hearts, and they aren't exactly hearts, they're specialized blood vessels that contract and push blood through the worm's body like a heart."

"Uhhh… okay. I'm sure you're right."

"And they also make the earth rich with nutrients for plants...with their poo!"

"That one I knew."

Asher felt, more than saw, a slight contraction from the earthworm. "Ooh! Dad, I think it's alive! Let's put it in the garden upstairs, in the tomato box. Maybe we'll grow better tomatoes."

"I like that idea. But we'd better hurry, I don't know if it'll live even if we put it in the garden. It's very dry."

"Alright." Asher ran before Ray could say anything more. He got to the door that led to the stairs up to their apartment and keyed in the code that unlocked it. The lock clicked open and he pulled at the handle. The door came flying open; seeing the door swing open so quickly, Ray was a little surprised at how strong his son must be getting. Ray caught up just before the door closed and latched. Asher ran up the stairs and tapped the black handle on a green wagon that sat next to the stairs. Ray was right behind and tapped the same handle. The wagon belongs to Simon and they tap it for good luck every time they walk by just as Simon had done.

Asher got to the top of the stairs, ran right by Mrs. Neighbors' open door and said "Hi, Mrs. Neighbors, gotta go. Gotta save a worm's life and grow big tomatoes." Alta Neighbors had grown accustomed to the odd things that came out of Asher's mouth and took him at his word that he was doing exactly that. She even thought that might be the same thing his mother would have done.

Asher put his lunchbox down, pulled his key from his pants pocket, and unlocked the door to his apartment to the left of the top of the stairs. Ray was only a couple of steps behind. He went to Mrs. Neighbors' open door and waved to her.

"Hi, Mrs. N. I'm going to make myself a sandwich and head on over to see Simon in a few minutes. Asher will be over soon to get your list."

Mrs. Neighbors was sitting in her avocado-green recliner enjoying the sun coming in her window as she watched a little bit of the afternoon soaps and game shows. When she spoke, you could hear her years of cigarettes and an exciting younger life in the sonorous, gravelly sound of her voice. "No worries. Good sun, good chair, bad back, bad hip—I'm not going anywhere." Truthfully, she was just glad to have friends that she could depend on and to whom she was able to give something in return. Without them, she would probably be in a nursing home or a bother to her granddaughter who was a busy, up and coming broadcast journalist for KCMW, the number-one local newscast. But with the Jakes just across the hall, she has been able to share her life with an adopted, extended family.

"Mrs. N. Do you know anything about...?"

"No son, I don't know." Alta Neighbors always called both Ray and Asher 'son'. "Frank just said that he might be selling and that he'd help me make other living arrangements if he did. I can tell that he's not so sure about this offer though. Something seems to nag at him about it."

"Well, you can come over tomorrow morning when Frank

comes up to tell me more. It'll save him some time anyway not having to explain it all twice." He paused and let the topic end itself. "I'll let you know when I'm on my way and I'll tell Asher to leave the door open so you two can hear each other."

"That'll be fine, son."

Ray gave a salutary nod of the head and turned away. He walked into the apartment with a "#3" in brass above the door. The living room was to the left as he stepped in, large but sparse and somewhat empty-looking with just a couch, loveseat, coffee table and small entertainment center. The wall facing the Park Blocks had a set of open sliding glass doors, allowing him to see Asher bent over a wooden, rectangular box, where Lynn had taught Asher to plant the tomatoes. There was a hallway to the right of the front door that led to two bedrooms, a bathroom, and a linen closet. Just on the other side of the hallway was the kitchen, also quite large for an apartment. It had a bar with stools on both sides, two on the living room side and two on the kitchen side. There was a chef's island in the middle of the kitchen. The apartment was originally designed as the residence for the owners of the building before the Harpers bought it, but that was many years and several renovations ago. Now it was just an unusually nice apartment.

Ray went into the kitchen and grabbed the makings for a turkey sandwich and got to work. He yelled over his shoulder, "Asher, you want a turkey sandwich?"

Thump, thump, thump. Asher came running in from the deck and jumped on a stool at the counter. "Yes, please. Only half."

"Got it. Would you mind going and snipping some oregano?"

"Okay." He jumped off the stool and ran out to the deck, then ran back into the kitchen. "Forgot the shears." He grabbed the kitchen shears from a countertop knife block and ran back outside. Lynn was the gardener. She had done a fine job of teaching Asher and Simon how to care for the garden they had put together on the deck.

After a few seconds, Asher was back with the oregano. According to Asher, anything from their garden always made their food taste better. Ray finely chopped the oregano and added it to the mayonnaise he had spread on the bread; this was something he had seen on a public television cooking show hosted by a very tall man with an English accent, glasses, and suspenders. He finished the two sandwiches and they sat and ate together, across the bar from each other with Asher in the living room. "Thanks Dad. Did you already see what J.J. has for the special tonight?"

"Chicken noodle with cheddar-garlic bread. I asked him when I went for breakfast this morning after dropping you and Lucie off at school. K.K. said she'd make you a fresh strawberry shake if you came tonight."

"Malt?"

"I don't know, you'll have to ask her when we get there."

Asher seemed to puzzle over something for a moment. "Do you think malt would be good with strawberry?" He asked as if it might be one of the most important questions he'd face any time soon.

"I think it would. My father would put malt on any ice cream or in any milkshake. I always liked it. I think maybe that's why you like malts so much; you probably got it from your grandfather."

"Really? Is that kind of thing genetic?"

"I don't know. It could be I suppose." Ray went on to tell his son a little more about his grandfather, who had passed away when Asher was only two years old, just months after Simon's birth. "My father didn't talk very much. He could hold a conversation if he wanted to, he just didn't. I think he thought that men were supposed to keep feelings inside, so I never knew much of what he was thinking unless I figured it out on my own, like the malt thing. So, when I see something like the fact that you like malt, it makes me feel like he shared that with you, and that makes it seem important."

"Yeah… I like that. I like malt like Grampa." Asher let the idea sink in. He knew that it was just as likely a coincidence as it was biological design, but for all the intellect that he had, he was still a sentimental being like both his mother and father. In the end, he decided that he got it from his grandfather.

They slowly ate their sandwiches in silence until Ray said "I need to go now. Leave the door open so you and Mrs. N. can hear each other, alright?" Ray picked up the last bit of his sandwich and headed toward the door.

"Got it under control, Dad." With each of them taking a final bite, Ray left the apartment to go see Simon and Asher scooted off the stool to go check in with Mrs. Neighbors.

The Painting Man and The Boy

The ladybug was about to pull at a weed in his bed of beef-steak tomato plants when the soil between the two rows of plants bulged upward a few inches. The soil cracked from whatever was coming through the ground. The ladybug grabbed his spade nearby and held it like an axe. He gritted his teeth and narrowed his eyes. His growling, rumbling voice bellowed as he spun his head sideways to the wizened moth perched on the stump by the side of the garden, "Get back Halfwing, I think they're coming up from the ground now."

The moth used its six legs to push backwards off the stump, one good wing and one bad wing furiously flapping. It watched the grizzled ladybug grip the spade in readiness to swing downward, but it sensed something. It saw a brown leathery mass, maybe eight or nine feet long and only eight or nine inches wide, wriggle up from the dirt. The moth sensed no threat and even sensed that this alien thing might need help. She looked at the ladybug and knew that he was about to swing the spade with his powerful arms. She still sensed something more. She sprung toward the ladybug. "Stop! Spots, stop!"

She landed in between Spots and the writhing, sickly thing. Spots was furious. "What are ya doin'?! I could'a killed ya. Get outta the way!" He didn't dare push at Halfwing, so he swiftly jumped over the aged moth, opened his wing case, buzzed his wings to maneuver around to get a safe angle at a rapid strike to the heart of the monster. He raised the spade high up and descended to his target with lethal intent. Spots brought down his spade and saw Halfwing lunge in front of his target to protect the thing; he attempted to alter the path of the spade but still clipped a wing of the moth, scales from the wing spraying into the immediate space in a dust cloud.

She stepped away from the flight of the spade and gave a soft, intensely restrained groan and looked up at Spots. Spots' eyes were wide and afraid for what he had done. "Stop!" She spoke this with sudden authority unchallenged.

"Halfwing, I'm sorry... I'm sorry," Spots dropped the spade, shock plastered on his face.

"Oh, stop it and help me with the worm. I'll be fine, you only nicked my bad wing. It won't slow me down any. I couldn't fly when I was only missing half of my wing; I'm sure that missing two-thirds won't make a difference." She looked at the horrified ladybug as she bent down to clear away some of the dirt from what she said was a worm. "Well! Get on with it, he's going to need your help. Let's find out what he might need."

Halfwing's tone and conviction shook Spots out of his stupor. He knew that Halfwing was certain of herself and that this worm was harmless. "Oh... uhh... hey buddy, you alright? Sorry 'bout tryin' to kill ya and everything. Can I get'cha somethin'? Are you hurt anywhere?" Spots wiped the dirt off the worm. It was clear now that this was certainly an earthworm, only with eyes, a nose, and ears on one end.

It spoke with a raspy and throaty sound in broken and fragmented words. "Water! Water, please! For me... the ground. Wet ground..."

Spots stood up and went to a well a couple dozen yards off to the side of a small grouping of huts. Halfwing was now holding the head of this worm in her lap and she wrapped her wings around him like a blanket.

The worm spoke again. "Water. Water… please… water."

"It's coming, dear. Spots will be back in just a moment. You just lay still and let me hold you. I'm keeping the wind off you with my wings." Halfwing watched the worm's breathing slowdown and his face relax. She had a special way of calming anyone and anything with her poised and motherly way.

Spots came buzzing back with two buckets full of water hanging below his gliding body and a ladle clanging about the side of one of the buckets. He dropped to his knees as he landed and immediately ladled some water and brought it to the lips of the worm who drank quickly. His eyes popped open and he looked at Spots with some unknown intent that put Spots back on the defensive. The ladybug was about to punch the worm between the eyes when the worm bent and curled and dove for one of the buckets. His head shot into the bucket with ferocity and within seconds the bucket was drained.

Spots was bewildered by what he saw but Halfwing just stood back, letting the worm fill its need.

Halfwing stepped next to Spots and spoke softly in his ear. "You did good, Spots. Thank you for protecting me and our home, but he's not from the Painting Man. He's from the boy."

He turned his head; his face told his surprise. "The boy? But we've only had vegetables and stuff like that from the boy." The two of them stepped back as the worm knocked over the remaining bucket of water and then rolled around in the wet ground, creating a slurry of mud. Rolling and twisting, he covered his body in the mud. "Thank you. I thank the two of you very much. Please, I need some more."

A few minutes passed as Spots and Halfwing brought water to the worm to drink and to make a mud pit for him. Soon the worm had collected himself, and though obviously weak and still needing recovery, was able to lay still and talk to the moth and ladybug.

It was Halfwing who started in. "Dear, you'll be safe here. Do you know who you are or what you are or how you got here?" He opened his mouth to answer the questions as naturally as you should answer such questions, but when there should have been sound, there was silence. His mouth hung open for a moment as his forehead wrinkled in perplexity. Finally, he spoke. "Well, it seems that I don't know."

Spots was stunned. "He *is* from the boy Halfwing, you were right. Hey worm, where were ya an hour ago, or yesterday? Ya don't know, do ya?" Spots stood up, filled with thrill. He spun away from the moth and worm and held a fist up toward some unseen, far off enemy. "We'll get ya, I know it. The boy's sendin' reinforcements now, ya piece o'..."

"Spots! Hush up. We have work to do and a new friend here to help. Go find Legs and Eyes and make a place for him to stay." Spots nodded to Halfwing in agreement and sped off.

"Excuse me... umm. Halfwing, is it? Who was the ladybug, uhh, Spots, yelling at?" The worm was confused and somewhat concerned. "It must be a terrible thing if Spots is speaking those words."

Halfwing gave a quick, almost imperceptible grimace before collecting her wits to speak. "Spots is a passionate being. Don't let him scare you. But there is a..." Halfwing thought for a moment, "...a danger. You'll be safe here where we are."

"What is the danger? I think I can help. If this will be my

home, I should help." The worm was implacable, needing to know more.

"There is someone we call the Painting Man. He doesn't bother us here but some of our friends have disappeared when wandering too far off toward his territory. He's a despotic tyrant to his people—I don't know if they should be called 'people'—followers, worshippers; 'prisoners' would be more appropriate. But the serious threat is that his reach is growing. It's growing slowly, but it's getting closer to us every day. We don't know how yet, but we have to find a way to stop him."

The worm was silent, mouth agape.

Halfwing sensed that fear was building inside the worm, now wondering just what fate had thrown at him. "It's okay, dear. You bring us hope, that's why Spots was so happy a moment ago. You're from the boy."

"The boy?"

"It's where you came from, it's where we all came from. We live in a place that is an existence created by the Painting Man, but also fueled by an opposing force to the Painting Man. That force is the boy, but we don't know quite how it all fits. He gave us the food we plant, it just started growing. It was only moments after we found ourselves here, as you just did, that Legs and Eyes—two others you'll meet—saw the food... a garden, actually."

"How do you know all of this?"

"I can sense it. I've always been able to sense it. I don't know how, but I just know and sometimes I even dream it. By the way, I should warn you that Legs and Eyes are spiders and quite large ones really."

"Who else is here? What else..."

Halfwing put the edge of her broken wing over the worm's

mouth. "Listen dear, you have to rest. I can tell that your body needs to recover, and your mind needs to settle. There is a place on the side of Spots' home that you can nestle into. It's protected by bushes and the ground stays moist there since the sun never hits it. You'll soon have your own place here; Legs and Eyes are very skilled builders." The worm took Halfwing at her word. Halfwing led as the worm contracted and expanded sections of his body to push himself forward as he followed.

*****

Asher went to his room after finishing his sandwich and hopped onto his bed. He reached up to an aluminum funnel that was sticking straight out of his wall from a hole. Attached to that funnel was a hose that stretched through the wall and down and over to the right about forty feet to where it entered the wall of Lucie's room downstairs behind Harper's Produce. In Lucie's room was an identical funnel. Asher called into the funnel, "Hey Lucie, you there?" His voice called brightly and loudly in Lucie's room. This 'telephone' was better than any tin-can-and-string contraption could ever hope to be.

Asher heard Lucie's voice clearly from his funnel. "Yeah, but I can't talk long. I have to go back to the kitchen to help my Mom with dinner. What d'you want?"

"My Dad and I are going to J.J.'s for dinner. Do you want to come along for some strawberry milkshakes?"

"Oh yeah!" she said with twelve-year old glee. "Come by and get me when you and your Dad go. Alright?"

"Okay. We'll be there after he gets back."

"'K. Gotta go, my Mom's calling me." Asher heard a clink through the funnel as Lucie let go of her end and her funnel was pulled to the wall by the weight of the hose. He let his funnel go and watched it do the same. Clink.

The Unexpectedly Active Mind

Ray sat down on the wooden chair next to Simon's medical bed. It had a seat cushion of vinyl over not-quite-enough padding. He waved goodbye to Cody. Cody was Simon's primary nurse in the long-term care facility where he'd been for the last year. Cody paused before leaving and asked, "Hey Ray, anything I can do for you?"

"Nah, just got some heavy thinking to do; I was hoping that talking to Simon would help," he responded with tight lips.

"Alright buddy, let me know when you leave." Cody closed the door behind himself to allow Ray his daily time with Simon.

Ray sat silently, leaning forward with his chin resting on his clasped hands and elbows on his knees. His eyebrows furrowed, and his jaw clenched. For many moments he sat there, just thinking about his home—their home—on the second floor of the Harpers' building. He forced the unpleasant thoughts out and looked over at his son. So young. Just ten years old and a bit small for his age. Simon was lying on his back; soon it would be time to turn him to a side. His white gown had baseballs and soccer balls and footballs stamped all over it, something that Asher and Lucie did one day as an homage to Simon's love of all sports with a ball. This gown was Ray's favorite part of the room, aside from Simon himself.

In fact, Ray hated much of the room. The monitors, breathing machine, cables, charts, clinically white tiles on the floor... he especially hated the sensors on Simon's head. There were eleven in all, all over his head, to read his brain activity. So many things in the room were some sort of reminder of the ever-present danger that his little boy was in.

Not all things in the room are what one would expect such things in a room to be. In particular, Simon's brain. It was active— inexplicably active. Nobody had answers for Ray. The activity said that Simon was hearing things, seeing things, feeling things, having emotions, and even developing new memories; yet, he *was* in a coma, or at least appeared to be in one. Ray chose to believe that all these indicators were good, and that Simon was still there; all evidence seemed to support this. Simon's condition was unique. But Ray still wanted his son to wake up more than anything else he could ever remember wanting. Ray hated those sensors that caused Simon's head to be shaved once every day; his hair was a shade darker than Lynn's hair, but just as thick and soft. Ray was thankful that the sensors showed that Simon's mind still worked very well, but he did hate them; they just didn't belong there.

Ray got up, walked around Simon's bed and went to the window and pulled open the curtains to let in the late day sun; Simon liked to play outside in the sun; he would often come home with his shirt and shoes off, prompting a search through the park. Ray would relive those memories every day that he opened the curtains.

Ray turned around to face the room. He saw that the small angel's wings on Simon's bed stand needed water. He got some from a sink on the wall on the opposite side of the room from Simon's bed and wetted the soil. Ray started to turn Simon on his side; this had to be done regularly to prevent bedsores and help blood flow. Ray turned Simon so that they would face each other when he sat back down, being careful not to detach any cords or sensors or tubes; he just hated those things. He adjusted Simon's tiny arms and legs so that his joints were bent in comfortable positions and no spots were taking too much pressure. Ray checked if Simon's nails needed to be trimmed and noticed that his hands were cold. So were his little feet. Ray adjusted the thermostat, then covered Simon with three special blankets. One was Simon's own, a white and purple, very-broken-in cotton baby blanket. Another used to be Lynn's baby blanket; it was cream satin on one side and faux fur on the other. And the last was Asher's baby blanket. It was the size of the other baby blankets but was covered in four-inch by four-inch drawings done in special crayons, permanently placed with an iron. This blanket was made by Lynn's one-time students when Lynn was pregnant with Asher. When Asher saw that Simon had their mother's blanket, Asher wanted Simon to have his as well.

"There you go, Simon." Ray ran his hand down Simon's cheek. As he looked at his son's still face, he thought about the sudden and scary news—they may have to move. They may have to leave the place that Ray and Lynn had turned into a home. This was the only place that Asher and Simon knew. What if Simon woke up and had to go home, only it wasn't home? It may just be out of Ray's hands; it was up to the Harpers. Ray sat and looked at Simon for a while—maybe two minutes, maybe twenty.

Asher could walk to PSU this summer for the science camps that the university puts on for elementary students. Lucie was always right next door. Truth be told, Ray had already thought about putting Simon into the Science camps too (when he woke up). "What do I do Sime?" Ray put his head down on the bed, right on Simon's hands and his eyes began to glisten. Ray put

Simon's hands between his own, looked up at his son and tried to pull himself together. "I'm sorry Sime, I shouldn't be like this." He didn't realize that this was bothering him so much. Ray shook his head to let out the tightness he was feeling and let out a weighted breath. He thought about how nice it was to have this time each day when he could focus himself and think about the heavier and harder things in life. "Boy, I want you back son." Ray shook his head again, this time pulling himself out of his funk. Seeing Simon usually put him at ease, and he was bringing himself to that place again, that place of unwavering faith that he found to be a grounding force, something he learned from Lynn. Even in death, she was his rock, his roots.

"Pull it together, Ray," he said out loud to himself. "There. I'm back, Sime. Hey, how about a song? I'll sing you one that I haven't sung in a while. It was your mother's favorite. It's called Arirang." Thinking back the many years to when he first heard Lynn singing the melody brought Ray refuge from the turmoil of the present. "Just in case you're really listening in there," (Ray was certain that he was) "it's about a man looking for someone he loves that has left to go back home. Arirang is a mountain pass he has to walk over to get back home to his love. The words kinda sound like his loved one left him or abandoned him, but really, they just parted ways for a little while, at least that's what I think. It's probably the most famous Korean song there is; your mother liked it for the melody, but I think it's a pretty story." Ray took a little breath and began:

Arirang, Arirang, Arariyo
I am crossing over Arirang pass.

The one who leaves me
Will not walk a mile before her feet hurt.

(Ray's voice cracked.)

Arirang, Arirang, Arariyo,
I am crossing over Arirang pass.
Just as there are stars in the sky,
There are many sorrows in my heart.

(Ray's hand has rested again on Simon's cheek, the outside
Of his thumb wet from wiping his eye.)

Arirang, Arirang, Arariyo
I am crossing over Arirang pass.
Over the mountain is my home,
Where, even into winters, flowers will bloom.

Although he finished the last verse, Ray kept humming the melody as he was stroking the back of Simon's ear. Images of Lynn long ago singing to their boys at bedtime drifting through his mind.

A Surprise for Mrs. Neighbors

Asher walked across the hallway to apartment #2 with thoughts of earthworms, malted milkshakes and earthworms *in* malted milkshakes, but he stopped that train of thought there as he wondered why the mind wanders in unexpected and tricky ways. With a turned stomach he knocked on Mrs. Neighbors' door. Her door was open so that she could hear him, but he knocked anyway out of respect and to let her know he was there.

"Hi, Mrs. N." Asher walked in and leaned against the wall near Mrs. Neighbors. Asher very much liked coming into Mrs. Neighbors' apartment. Although she kept it clean, it had that musty smell that only comes with age, old leather, old books and paper, and old pictures. The only new item in the room was a thirty-two-inch television with a remote control. "It's important to do the things right in life that you enjoy…" says Mrs. N., who likes television maybe a little too much; besides, it allowed her to see her granddaughter more clearly during the newscasts.

Mrs. Neighbors turned off her television with the remote, sat back in her avocado-green, poofy chair and said to the boy, "All done with the sixth grade? Think you're ready to move on?"

"Yes. Sixth grade was pretty boring. I mean, I had fun with Lucie, but the school stuff was boring."

"Well son, I think you'll always find your schooling boring.

When they made those curriculums, they didn't make them for you. Or is it 'curricula'?"

"Curricula. I know, that's what Mrs. Good told me too, but last year... everyone just treated me weird." Asher looked out the nearby window.

"It's alright son; that'll probably never change either while you're in school. The teachers will always know that you lost your mother, and they'll know the situation with your brother and people won't quite know how to deal with that. And your classmates will always find out and ..." she reached out and touched Asher's chin, gripping his attention and lowering her voice. "I don't mean to force you to grow up before your time, but your father and Lucie and I will be here to keep you sane, child, and in school and places like that, you'll have to be the strong one. It isn't fair, but it's how it's got to be." She kept intense eye contact with Asher and although her words were painful, they were also caring. Whenever she spoke like this, her words seemed to sink in deeper than when anyone else spoke to him, embossing on leather instead of ink on paperboard. They were hard words to accept, but when coming from Mrs. Neighbors, he *could* accept them.

"Thanks." He looked back at Mrs. Neighbors then toward the table. "Uh, where's your shopping list?"

"That's right," she rolled her eyes at the absent-mindedness, "I was writing it but got caught up in my soap." She produced a slip of paper and a pencil from the space between the arm of the chair and her leg and wrote something on it then handed it to Asher. "Simple list today, son. Thank you."

Asher grabbed it and ran without even looking at the list; he had a pretty good idea what was on it. "I'll be back soon, Mrs. N."

"Wait a second! An old lonely lady like me likes a little more

43

conversation, son. You should know that about people and act accordingly."

"I'm sorry, Mrs. N." Asher returned to the same place, leaning once again on the wall right by her chair. "I'm just ready to go running around. But I can talk too; I like talking to you."

"Of course you like talking to me, I'm terrific company. No doubt you're full of energy from going to Bruno's." A wry smile crept across Alta Neighbors' face.

"Probably...wait! How'd you know?!"

She put her thumb to her tongue then said as she reached for Asher, "You have a spot a bit above your eyebrow. How'd you get it there?" She rubbed the chocolate spot away with her moist thumb.

Embarrassed, Asher responded, "...umm, I don't know, maybe Lucie did it."

"Oh, I doubt that son. I've had my own children besides you and your brother; the mess a child makes... I swear..."

"Yeah, you're probably right, but it was delicious, so I don't mind. Hey, Mrs. N., what's your favorite flavor?"

Mrs. Neighbors settled back into her chair, that last question pulling her into an old memory. "Pistachio. A long time ago when my husband was still alive, we would share pistachio ice cream and coffee. He used to distract me then steal bites out of my bowl. Mr. Neighbors wasn't very neighborly when it came to pistachio ice cream, but I didn't mind. I always dished more than I could eat knowing he would eat at least half of it himself."

"He sounds fun. I hope to be like that when I grow up."

"Don't you dare go stealing your wife's ice cream!" said Mrs. Neighbors with a stern glare.

Asher stood silently, wondering if he was really in trouble.

"Ha…," bellowed Mrs. Neighbors as she clapped her hands, "don't worry son, I was just teasing, I know what you meant. You're a good soul like your mother is."

Asher heard Mrs. Neighbors use the word "is" instead of "was" and it struck him. He felt the word as much as he heard it; just the same way Mrs. Neighbors spoke a few minutes ago. It made him feel safe and warm thinking of his mother as an "is" instead of a "was."

"Son, son?" Alta Neighbors snapped her fingers in front of Asher's eyes to get his attention. "Where'd you go son? You sort of drifted off, was it a daydream? It had to have been a good one. Want to tell me about it?"

Asher's face felt warm to him as it flushed red, just a little embarrassed but comfortable enough in front of Mrs. Neighbors. "You just made me think about my mom, the way you said 'she is' instead of 'she was.' If other people talk about her, they always talk about her in the past tense. But you didn't. It just made me think." Asher didn't know why he explained all that to her. If someone else asked him a question like that he would have just brushed them off and pretended it was nothing.

"Well son, she *is* an *'is'*. Don't you know that?"

The way that Mrs. Neighbors stared at him so intently as she spoke filled Asher with the confidence that he did indeed thoroughly understand exactly what Mrs. Neighbors had told him. He nodded and said to her, "I guess you're telling me what my dad says too, that my mom's in the person that I am and, in our family, because she helped to make us who we are."

Alta Neighbors put a hand on Asher's knee, "and don't you forget it." Then she winked at him. "Thank you, son, for indulging a lonely old lady in some idle chit-chat. Run along now. I'm not going to live forever, I'm eighty-two years old. You hurry back, alright?"

Asher shook his head as he thought about Mrs. Neighbors telling him to hurry along after being the one who asked him to stay and talk. He jumped up and ran out the door. When Asher got to the bottom of the stairs he stopped and finally looked at the list to figure out his route for the day. He read the list, grabbed the wagon, and headed out the door.

Alta Neighbors listened to Asher's clomping footsteps; after a few seconds, the door at the bottom of the steps opened and then closed. "Yes son, thank you very much for talking to me." She stood up and turned toward her door, looking past it, seeing apartment #3 across the hall. She stared at that door as if trying to see beyond it. She walked slowly toward it without breaking her gaze. As Alta Neighbors reached her destination, she tilted her head as if to listen into apartment #3 then raised both hands to the door at face-level, put the side of her head on the door and closed her eyes. Alta Neighbors stood there for several long moments pressed against the door to the apartment where Asher and Ray lived. Her breathing quickened, and she started to mumble in hushed tones. Her head snapped back, and her eyes popped open, mouth agape. "Oh, my lord…oh dear." She quickly turned and went back into her apartment, left the television off and sat for a long time in her chair, biting her thumb, her face fixed in a mix of concern and unknown intent staring at the space of nothing in front of her.

The Tomato Planter Box

Soda crackers
Tomato soup
Small brisket
1 cabbage
2 onions
Bag of carrots
Lighter
Paper towels
TV Guide
Drawing paper
Small bag of potting soil from Mrs. Lownsdale

Asher had to run quickly north along the park blocks to get the soil from the park's gardener, Mrs. Lownsdale, before she left for the day. Mrs. Neighbors and she have been friends for many, many years. They had been in similar social circles in past decades and until the last couple of years, Mrs. Neighbors would occasionally help Mrs. Lownsdale in the gardens of the Park Blocks, both ladies as volunteers. Now that Mrs. Neighbors has too much difficulty physically, she's bound to just keeping a few plants in her apartment, and a couple of times a year will re-pot them.

Asher pocketed the list and headed to the park gardens to the north with Simon's wagon in tow. Asher didn't mind doing this for Mrs. Neighbors the two or three times a week that he did. It was, however, the most difficult part of his day. Asher used to often do this with Simon and the two of them would have the kinds of conversations that brothers of their ages would have. "He-Man is so strong, I bet he's stronger than the Incredible Hulk," Asher would say, then Simon would argue the point since they were brothers, and it was practically his job to do so. "No way! Hulk can make a storm from clapping his hands and if He-Man makes him mad, he's just gonna get even stronger!" And so on.

Many days, the two boys would have races, Asher pulling the wagon to even things up and (of course) Simon would win every time. Sometimes Asher would pull Simon in the wagon when his little brother was tired and sometimes Simon would pull Asher in the wagon when he was trying to be big and strong.

There was one day in late fall prior to the summer of the accident that Simon noticed a butterfly—or what he thought was a butterfly—on the side of a tree trunk. Asher corrected him and explained that it was a moth. "You can tell because the moth has wings that lay down flat and a fat and hairy body with shorter legs and if you look at the antennae it looks like a small feather instead of thin and like the handle of a baseball bat at the end."

And right on cue Simon found an argument: "But you said that moths are out at night and butterflies are out during the day. You told me that remember?"

"Yeah, I remember." Asher was a little frustrated. Why must Simon always argue? Simon felt a little victory. "But Simon, look closely at it, it's resting. It has to sleep somewhere in daytime and see how it's camouflaged on the tree, you only saw it because we were so close."

Simon's expression fell a little bit. "Oh, so it is a moth?"

"Yes, just look at its body, you can tell. Besides, I know I told you that moths are nocturnal, and butterflies are diurnal but there are a couple of moths that are diurnal, and many are crepuscular too."

"Crap- what?"

"Hmm… ok, listen Simon. Nocturnal means awake at nighttime. Diurnal means awake at daytime. *Creh-pus-cue-lur* means awake when the sun is setting and rising and asleep when it's totally day and totally night. That means that you can see those moths when the sun is in the sky as long as it's low in the sky. Look at where the sun is; it'll be down in maybe an hour." Asher couldn't help it; his tone of voice was demeaning to his baby brother. *But it was Simon's fault for arguing* he told himself.

"Scra-puckler?" Simon tried the new word out, knowing that Asher was probably right about everything he said.

"Creh - pus - cue - lur."

"Crap-puscular—that's what I said!" They both let the argument drop and Simon immediately shouted "1-2-3-GO!!!" to start a race knowing he would win and have his moment to shine. By the time Asher figured it out and started running, pulling the heavy John Deere wagon behind him, Simon was easily seven or eight strides ahead. Asher really didn't mind because Simon was easily the better athlete, even at two years younger. It wasn't so much that Asher was "the smart one" and Simon "the athlete"; Simon was very intelligent, maybe as intelligent as Asher, it's just that Asher was fervent for knowledge and searched out and sucked up information like a giant vacuum at a dust-bunny convention; Simon had yet to find that thirst outside of sports and games.

As Asher was thinking back on the particular moment when he and Simon were toting the very same wagon he had today, he realized he was standing now in front of Mrs. Lownsdale; his thoughts had made the walk fly by.

"Hello dear, what can I do for you?" Mrs. Lownsdale had taken on a bit of a tremor in her voice and Asher wondered if she would have to quit tending these gardens soon like Mrs. Neighbors.

"Mrs. N. needs some soil." He didn't say it in a surly way, but Mrs. Lownsdale did give him a look of reprimand.

"Asher, don't you let yourself fall into a melancholy now. It's a beautiful day and no doubt you must be glad to have the summer."

"Yeah, I guess Mrs. Lownsdale." Asher forced a smile. "It's going to be a fun summer. Lucie and I have big plans." They had no plans.

"Alright then, which plant is it?" she said as she brushed her hands on an apron and got ready to grab one of four different soil mixtures.

"Umm, I don't know but I think it's the one with the dark purplish leaves that have the silver spots." For all the knowledge Asher had about animals, he had no interest in plants except for the trees in the Park Blocks, for which he did take the time to learn each of the species and the ones in his mother's garden that he still tended every day.

"That's the angel-wing begonia she asked for last year. It's a hardy, tropical plant so this bag will do just fine." She grabbed a white plastic bag that had the words "general potting" written in permanent marker on the outside; it was her own mixture, which was appropriate since Mrs. Lownsdale was a Master Gardener. She handed the bag to Asher who put it in the wagon.

"Thank you, Mrs. Lownsdale."

"You're as welcome as the birds in May, my dear. Please say 'hi' to Alta for me."

"Sure will! Have a nice day!!" Asher made the point to sound cheery. Asher left and made his way to all the necessary locations finishing with Harper's Produce and then back upstairs.

It took three trips up and down the stairs to get everything into Mrs. Neighbors' apartment. She was asleep in her chair, so Asher tried his best to let her sleep, only waking her momentarily to let her know that he had put everything away for her.

"Thank you, son" she said in the somewhat slurred voice of someone waking before they should.

"You're welcome. I'm going to go across the hall and read for a while until I go get my dad. Okay?" He waited for her to respond.

"Umm… Asher?"

"Yes, Mrs. N., are you okay?" Asher got down on a knee, partly in deference but also to look closely at Alta Neighbors.

"I'm okay son. Asher, why don't you get your book and come back over here so I can keep a good eye on…" a pause, her expression betrayed intense thought, "…wait, better yet son, you can stay over there, let me just come over and move around for a bit. I've been stuck in this chair for far too long today."

"Alright Mrs. N." Asher thought he heard something peculiar in her voice, a concern maybe, one that normally wasn't there, but the thought passed since she did like to get up and move around sometimes and he wanted to go and read his book anyway. It was an Isaac Asimov story; Asimov was his favorite author.

They both headed across the hall and upon entering the Jakes' apartment, Alta Neighbors just stood there, barely in the door, surveying the place. Asher ignored her, going to his room to read his book on his bed next to an open window. Mrs. Neighbors took a few steps into the apartment then looked left toward the garden on the deck. She moved with resolve—or at least as much resolve as a hobbled eighty-two-year-old could gather. She got to the glass and looked out into the garden, eventually settling her attention on the raised box of tomato plants. With all her awareness focused on the contents of that box, she let her eyes roll back into her head, lids closed. After several seconds she opened her eyes and turned away from the door. "Asher. Come here son, I'd like to talk to you for a minute."

Asher came bounding out from his room, a finger holding his place in his book. "Yeah, Mrs. N.?"

"Tell me son, what was it you said to me earlier today when you first got home from school?"

Asher was puzzled. "Uhh... I don't remem... oh yeah, the worm, I was saving a worm's life, I put it in the tomato planter box. It needed moisture 'cause it was getting dry on the sidewalk. Maybe I should go put more water in the dirt." Forgetting that Mrs. Neighbors was attempting a dialogue, Asher started to step toward the kitchen, only to be stopped by a remarkably strong grip on his shoulder.

"Hold on, son. You put the worm in the tomato box? Are you sure?"

"Yes, I'm sure. Is something wrong?" Asher didn't understand this line of questioning at all. He saw Mrs. Neighbors turn her head toward the planter box that they were discussing and stare at it for a moment, shoulders scrunched and an occasional slight movement of her head as if she were trying very hard to listen to something and the minor tilts and turns brought it into focus.

After a long moment, Mrs. Neighbors relaxed, turned back to the confused little boy, and smiled reassuringly, "No, nothing is wrong at all. In fact, I think you are right; it could use some more water. It looks like our late spring sun is potent. You take good care of that soil and that worm. In no time, you'll see a sea of blooms on those plants!"

"Yes Mrs. N.!" She watched him retrieve a watering can and wet the soil. She could tell that he felt like he did something right by saving the life of a poor worm, dying slowly on a hot, dry cement sidewalk. She was only a little bit afraid as she stood there, watching him, thinking about what he had really done by placing the worm in that particular planter box with that particular purpose. She would have to watch him much more closely now. She has waited many years for this time and now he's taken his first step on a path he never imagined.

They Set a Trap

Spots sat with clenched fists as he heard the news from Eyes and Legs. Legs speaking now, "They're gone. The Painting Man's soldiers had set a trap and it killed two of the ants. They also captured one other with the same trap and they took him."

"Who was it they took?"

"Leaf. He was clueless. They put a packing-cloth over his head before he even knew what was happening." Legs' hard-edged voice was very matter-of-fact. Spots already knew that Legs was planning to rescue Leaf.

Spots was worried for the other two ants. "Who died?"

Legs spoke again. "Red and Fiveleg."

Eyes spoke with a quaver in her voice. "Blue and her children are going to be devastated. Blue always hated when Red went out on patrol; she might be angry with us for his death."

Spots spoke up, "Halfwing'll talk to her. She'll help Blue to understand that Red died doing the best he could protectin' their children. Fiveleg's brothers and sisters will be proud o' him. Their deaths ain't gonna count for nothin'."

A Pretty Melody

Asher had a difficult time putting his book down, but it was 6:15 and time to get his father. He let Mrs. Neighbors know he was leaving and found her in his own living room on the love seat by the window instead of in her own apartment like usual watching her favorite game show, the one with the dragon hidden on the tic-tac-toe board. She had been napping. He hadn't seen her do that before in his own apartment and wondered why she stayed there this time. He woke her and then headed out of the apartment. Mrs. Neighbors followed, closing and locking the door behind her as she went across the hall.

Mrs. Neighbors called after Asher, "You be careful son while you're out there on your way to get your father."

This was also odd to Asher. Mrs. Neighbors hadn't said something like that to him in years; she had learned that he was capable, careful, and wary a long time ago and didn't demean him by saying something that would assume he was anything other. But he didn't know how to ask her if she was ok or if everything was alright without feeling awkward. He let it drop and settled on shouting back that he'd be safe and ran down the stairs and out to the sidewalk, nearly tripping over a black-and-grey stray tabby cat that sat just a foot away from the door on the sidewalk. Asher hadn't seen this cat around here before, but he had no time to stop now so he suppressed his urge to bend down and try to pet it.

The sunlight came through the trees from the west to dapple on the east side of the Park Blocks as he continued on his way. The sun falling in this way always brought him to reminisce about summers past playing in the Park Blocks with Simon and Lucie. He thought about all the adventures he and Lucie could have this summer. Imaginary play was still common with these two. Often, they would go treasure hunting; sometimes it was "save Princess Lucie" or "save Prince Asher" if Lucie was feeling plucky and pushy. Recently Asher had been coming up with an imaginary character, the prince of a land made of candy and toys, who had been kidnapped by the Lord of Lost, a mean man who takes the candy and toys from happy children. But at twelve years of age now, these games felt a little childish—the pull to play these games equally countered by the desire to discover what it meant to be too old to play them.

With thoughts of himself and Lucie off saving this-and-that, he walked to the corner of the Harper's block. He went north across the street to then turn right and walk parallel to Harper's Produce, the sun now warming his back. He soon reached a wooden building halfway down the block with dark brown trim on light tan walls and eves projecting a German or Swiss chalet design that stood out from the concrete, glass, metal, and stucco of the more modern Portland buildings adjacent. The out of place building was a carriage house converted to a long-term care clinic that Ray could not pass up, being only barely more than one block away from the Jakes' apartment and directly across the street from the entrance to Harper's Produce. Again, Asher thought of the Harper mantra, "everything in walking distance…"

The clinic was an extension of Oregon Health and Sciences University. OHSU was a leading research institution in all things medical and had several satellite clinics to house the growth it had experienced in the last decade. Asher entered the clinic ignoring the sign stating that visiting hours were over and waved to Cody, who was sitting behind the reception desk.

"Hey Asher, your dad's a little down today. Is he alright?"

"I think so; I think it's just 'cause it's been almost a year now since it happened."

"Yeah, it has been, hasn't it? I'm sorry buddy. How ya doin'?"

"I'm okay. My dad and I take care of each other pretty well so we're fine. I'm gonna go and wait for him."

Asher walked back to Simon's room and sat on a small seat attached to the wall just outside the door. He leaned his head back to rest on the wall, just inches from the door and noticed that his father was humming a song. He remembered the melody. His mother would sing it to him in bed as a young child when he was upset about something-or-other, sobbing uncontrollably, until she sang this very melody. He didn't remember any words; did his mother sing words? Or did she just hum? Maybe it was some kind of nonsense lyric. *Ariarian*? Yes, *Arrirang*. And he heard his father sing those very syllables. "Arrirang, Arrirang, Arrariyo."

Asher started to hum the melody to himself and just enjoy the song. All by itself, it was such a pretty melody. He was interrupted by his father opening the door so he stopped his singing, pretending he had just been sitting there waiting.

"You ready, Dad? We have to stop by the Harper's and get Lucie before we go to J.J.'s."

"Sounds good. I'm hungry anyway. You?" Ray put a quick sleeve up to dry his cheek. His eyes were red-rimmed and bloodshot, and his lashes clumped together, still a little wet; both he and Asher ignored that Asher had noticed.

"Yeah Dad. Starving. And besides, I really wanna try that strawberry malt."

"Uh-huh. It does sound good." Ray paused a moment, searching futilely for more to say without treading in waters too deep. "Well Simon looks healthy."

"Good."

The two walked in silence to the Harper's building.

The Disconnects

J.J.'s Diner was a simple, but to the point setup. J.J.'s was not a true diner, or at least not in the truest sense of the word since it was not a converted railcar, but it was set up about the same. Instead of booths, J.J.'s had eight round tables, the first just as you walk in the door, one in the near corner and the other six lined up between a bar and a wall of large windows. Some of the patrons were watching a television that was mounted on the wall above the end of the bar that was near the entrance.

Lucie burst through the front door but after two steps she stopped, almost plowing straight into J.J. himself, whose arms were filled with dirty plates, glasses of half-drunk sodas, and too much silverware to count. The glare that the daunting man gave Lucie sent the exact message he desired. She turned her head down and walked, hands clasped together, to their usual table in the close corner and kept her lips tightly shut. Asher walked in quietly after witnessing the close call and went and sat down next to Lucie while Ray apologized to J.J.

"'S'alright Ray, but keep an eye on those two; I'm not up for any of those silly, little tricks they try pulling on me all the time." With his arms growing tired, he stomped away behind the counter and toward the dish-room.

Ray sat down by the two children, "I think he's a bit grumpy today, what do you think?"

"Uhh-huh!!" said Asher as he nodded emphatically.

"Well Mr. Jakes, he *is* awake you know."

"Yeah Dad, the world is still turning…"

"And I haven't seen pigs flying today either!"

"Stop it you two." Ray said this a little too harshly since usually he would join in on the jibing of his good friend. "I'm sorry. I've got a lot on my mind. Why don't we get to ordering, do you two want the special too?"

As Asher nodded, Lucie said "I ate already. Just dessert for me." And just like clockwork K.K. showed up by the table. "Hi, sweeties! What's for dinner?" K.K. was J.J.'s daughter, and in most ways the opposite of her father. She was about as cheery as a puppy waking from a good nap ready to pounce on her still-sleeping siblings.

"Asher and I are having the chicken noodle and cheesy garlic bread. Lucie is here for dessert later but I'm sure she'd also like some garlic bread." The children nodded, obviously working hard at staying quiet for the moment.

K.K. leaned close to the children and whispered to them, "Don't let my dad scare you. He's really a softy. I just ignore him or tease him most of the time and then he leaves me alone."

A disembodied voice from the dish-room came calling "Katherine Kelly, I need more dishes back here; get those tables cleaned up out there."

"Okay Pop!!" K.K. made a mocking grouch face toward Asher and Lucie as she sped past to clean up a table and they had to cover their mouths to keep from laughing too loudly.

After a few minutes, they were served and were eating. Everything that J.J. made was delicious. The man may not be particularly good with customers, but he was a wonder at a stove. K.K. was nearly as talented as her father in the kitchen, but also a charm with the customers.

It was when they had been eating for a while that Asher began to notice that most of the people in there were staring at a news report that was on the television. Asher looked up to the T.V. mounted on the wall and recognized Mrs. Neighbor's granddaughter, who was also a close friend of the Jakes family, speaking.

> "...this is the third report this week of someone being found in a catatonic state or 'state of disconnect' as it's being called by OHSU doctors. For those of you who haven't been following this story, it started about six months ago when two men and one woman were found sitting on the ground by the Ira Keller fountain completely uncommunicative. EMS responded and they have been up at OHSU since then. Doctors and police are baffled. Since that day, more people, between one and two a week, have been found in and around Portland in this exact state. Doctors do not know exactly what this is; it's different from anything they have come across before. Matthew Maxwell is with Dr. Paul Britton at OHSU to get deeper into this story. Matthew, share with us some information you've gotten from Dr. Britton.
>
> "Thank you, Jenny. Dr. Britton, can you explain anything to us about these cases, what they have in common, if you've discovered a source, a cause or a treatment?"
>
> "Well, unfortunately we have little more to say than what we've already shared with you. Each one of these cases from the beginning is nearly identical. All the people were found outdoors, awake but uncommunicative. Oddly, these people can respond to questions or commands of the very

basic, 'stand', 'sit' etcetera, they can eat, get dressed, relieve themselves, all of the very basic things we do to survive, but anything of higher brain functions is simply not there."

"So, can they answer simple questions like 'what's your name?'"

"They cannot in fact. In the simplest of terms, they are a functional body without a person inside. That's why we're calling them 'disconnects" instead of labeling them as catatonic. In a state of catatonia, a person is completely non-functioning and that's not the case here. It's not something we have seen before at this frequency. They appear unharmed, at least physically."

"Thank you, Dr. Britton, for your candor. Tell us, you brought up the subject of the frequency of these cases, how many have there been since the first ones found at the Keller fountain back in December?"

"There have been forty-three. That number is shocking—it's well beyond coincidence. But I assure you and the Portland public, we are doing everything we can to discover the cause. We have even enlisted the help of the CDC. Their resources have quadrupled our field investigations to find possible causes."

"Is it communicable?"

"No, it is not, at least not from person to person."

"Is it becoming more frequent?"

"The cases have been appearing at a clip of just more than one a week until this week when three appeared. It's too early to say whether it's just an anomaly or an indicator of a true increase in appearances. I'm sure we'll soon find out though."

"Thank you again, Dr. Britton. Back to you Jenny."
"Thank you, Matthew. In Portland Trail Blazers news…"

Everyone in the diner started talking after the report. Lucie and Ray were engrossed in a conversation of their own about the spaghetti sauce she just learned to make from her mother. Asher listened to the people in the diner and heard various opinions come through.

"I bet that it's in the Willamette River water, they're probably getting too close to it or falling in and a week later this happens. That river is full of pollution, you know it…"

"It's computers, they're killing brain cells and taking people's free will, there's one in every one-hundred homes now, and I betcha each one of them folks is from one of those homes…"

"It's the Russians…"

"People just are too lazy today; they just lay around and then eventually they can't do anything."

Asher didn't know what it was, but he knew enough to be quite certain that all of those things were wrong.

Asher looked down and noticed that he had forgotten to eat and both Ray and Lucie were nearly done. Asher ate quickly; mainly, he hurried because he knew that a strawberry milkshake was on the way, maybe with malt if he remembers to ask K.K., before she brings them out. Luckily for him, she was soon by the table, clearing it and asking them if they'd like any special treatment to their shakes or a particular ice cream.

"What would you like, kiddos? We've got fresh vanilla, chocolate or creamy custard, all from Bruno's and the strawberries are from your dad, Lucie."

Lucie jumped in her seat, "Ooh they are soooooo gooooood!! I snuck some from the flats this morning. Oops!" she put her hand to her mouth to shush herself "...please don't tell my dad. He hates it when I do that." The other three were not surprised. She burst out once again with lightning speed "Creamy custard and can you put some peaches in it too, please?"

"I surely can ma'dear and I promise not to tell your dad." K.K. let a quick scribble fall onto her little order pad.

"Asher? Ray? Anything special for you?"

Asher went first, "I'd like the strawberries in the creamy custard too, and with malt if you have some, please."

"I'll have it that way too. Thanks K.K." said Ray.

"I'll have those right up." Again, with a couple of quick scribbles, she turned toward the kitchen and cleared off two tables on the way. J.J. turned the "OPEN" sign off and just to make sure no one came in after this, he also put up a "Closed" sign on a stand and put it in front of the door. This clued the rest of the customers to finish up and clear out.

Ray crossed his arms on the table and rested his chin on them to be head-level with the two children and said "So, what do the two of you have planned for tomorrow?"

Lucie spoke first, "We talked about it today at school. We're going to go get some stuff from Mrs. Lownsdale and work up in the garden and try to grow some new things but I don't remember what... oh yeah, sunflowers and something else and then we're going to go to the fountain and listen to the guys that like to play the guitar there and then we're going to go play games at my house but first, and Asher doesn't know this yet, I'm going to feed him spaghetti and he better like it or else..." she finally took a deep breath "… I'm going to be mad at him all day!"

"I don't have anything else to add to that, Dad." said Asher.

"Well I should hope not, I won't get to see you at all if you try to add anything to that itinerary." Asher and Ray both laughed at Lucie who just sat there confused. Lucie looked between the two of them.

"What? …What?! Never mind. I was thinking Asher, we could even go to Powell's and start our summer reading list and you know I was thinking maybe ten or twelve books would be good this summer cause I really wanted to read "A Wrinkle In Time" again and then read more "Black Beauty" books but I also wanted to read some of your Isaac Asimov books you always talk about but I never could read them and I was thinking that maybe I can read them now 'cause my mom and my dad both say I'm more patient than I used to be and it's 'cause Mrs. Good did such a good job helping me learn… WAIT!! Mrs. Good … good teacher!! That's funny! But anyway, she said I learned how to wait or something but what do they know 'cause I bet it's just because I'm older now, right?"

"Yup, right." Asher was used to his best friend's break-neck delivery of verbiage.

Lucie said "Exactly! That's what I tried to tell them but they just don't believe that I could learn to be patient all on my own without help from… STRAWBERRY MILKSHAKE!!" The last two words were squealed more than they were spoken.

Both J.J. and K.K. were now delivering the shakes in tall fountain glasses, with whipped cream on top and with thick straws. There were five in total; it was common that J.J. and K.K. would sit with Asher and Ray if they were the last two in the diner. "Here ya go, kids," said J.J. as he lowered their shakes, "Yours with peaches,

Lucie, and yours with malt," he said to Asher. "You're going to love 'em kids, Bruno knows how to make his stuff—I tell ya."

"Sooooo delicious!" Lucie said with a mouthful of milkshake.

For a moment all was quiet as the five of them enjoyed their desserts. J.J. spoke first. "Excellent work, Katherine Kelly."

"Thanks Pop." K.K. gave her father a hug around his arm. K.K. was a student at the Western Culinary Institute. She had lofty goals of owning her own restaurant that would specialize in Northwest cuisine. J.J. had faith in his daughter and he had every reason to believe she would achieve her goal.

Asher turned to K.K. and asked "Hey K.K., why does J.J. call you that instead of K.K.? OH!! J.J. and K.K. - I just got it! It's in alphabetical order!"

J.J. responded before K.K. could answer. "It's because Katherine Kelly is the name I gave her. I don't care what you call her but I'm going to call her Katherine Kelly."

K.K. said under her breath to Asher and Lucie, "Honestly kids, I have no idea why he calls me 'Katherine Kelly' but I like that he does."

"So why do you go by K.K. the rest of the time?" said Asher.

"Well my teachers when I was really young would call me Katherine or Kathy instead of Katherine Kelly, so I asked them to call me K.K. instead because our family has always done names that way. My granddad was Ian Isaac and my great granddad was Hampton Henry. My granddad used to tell me that Frederick Franklin wasn't very smart because he named his own son Gerald Gerald."

Both children gave a chuckle then Asher changed subjects, "K.K., this is so yummy. Will you teach me how to make milkshakes like this?"

"I sure can, sweetie." She reached over with a napkin that came out of her apron and dabbed a spot of whipped cream that found its way to just above and behind the apple of Asher's cheek.

The talk slowed down as they all finished up their shakes. The little talk that remained was dominated by the subject of Lynn Jakes. This group had finished the sad way of talking about Lynn many months ago and they just fondly reminisced. It was Simon whom they rarely talked about—it pained Ray too much.

The five of them eventually got up to turn all the chairs upside down on the tables so that J.J. and K.K. could go about the business of cleaning.

After goodbyes, Asher and Ray walked Lucie home and then went upstairs. The black-and-gray stray tabby was at the door as they entered their building and Asher bent down this time to pet it and it obliged the brief touch. They tapped the handle to the green John Deere wagon as they started up the stairs.

"You know what, Dad? I really did like the malt in the strawberry shake."

Ray bent over and kissed the top of his son's head. "Me too."

*****

Halfwing, Spots, Legs, and Eyes were sitting around a small fire, discussing the state of affairs and the dangers they faced, as the worm wriggled his way into the small circle.

He looked at them all and asked what they were talking about and if he could help.

Spots spoke up, "Sure, you could help! But what can you do?"

Halfwing interrupted, "Spots is right, you can help, but you need to understand that we face a terrible monster in the Painting

Man. He has lookouts posted all around his hold. We can't get close enough to really see what's going on in there. We've tried but two of our own have died doing so."

The worm spoke again, "I understand, but I feel like I should be able to do something. What do you need help with?"

Eyes spoke this time; as the more vocal of the two spiders, her father was usually content to let her speak, "We don't really know without getting a closer look. The ants tried to get close and they were killed and captured. My father and I tried to get close through the treetops, but we discovered that the Painting Man has them all cut down from at least 200 yards away. We don't have a way in."

The worm wriggled with excitement, "I CAN GET IN!!! I'll go through the ground!" With that, he dove headfirst and dug faster than imaginable. He was gone in seconds and reappeared fifteen feet away through the ground. "Umm… where am I going?"

Spots said, "I think we'll call him Digger."

Legs gave the solution. "Eyes and I will weave him a basket and we'll carry him through the treetops until we can't go any farther. He'll be able to see where he needs to go by that point."

Halfwing smiled and told her friend, "Legs, that is an excellent idea. The Boss would approve."

The worm, now Digger, asked, "Who's this boss?"

Eyes explained to Digger, "He has become our leader in trying to keep our home protected and in going out to scout the lands of the Painting Man."

Spots spoke up now, "He's pretty good at that sorta stuff. He thinks of it like a game and everything's been fine until the two ants were killed. He went out alone this time; Legs made him a suit from his silk and stuck twigs and leaves all over so that he could stay hidden."

"What's the boss's name?" Digger asked.

Halfwing explained, "his name is Boss. He didn't have a name until we discovered that he knew how to take charge of things and so we called him 'Boss'."

Digger asked, "Will I get to meet him soon—show him that I can be helpful?"

Halfwing nodded, "He'll be back soon I'm sure; he never leaves us here for more than a day or two. You'll like him very much."

Legs began to crawl away, "Let's get moving, if we can have you back by the time the Boss gets back, we might be able to make some kind of plan to rescue Leaf."

Asher Dreams of Bugs

When Asher and Ray entered the apartment, Ray went to one end of the bar where a typewriter sat, to work on a column he'd been tinkering with for the Oregonian and Asher went outside to tend to the garden. He didn't water in the evening; Lynn had taught him that plants are more likely to get diseased when watered at night.

Asher spent most of his time this evening by tending to the tomato plants. He grew several cherry tomatoes and the San Marzano variety of Romas. Mr. Harper shared with Lynn several years ago that the San Marzano Roma tomato was the best tomato for Italian cooking and tomato sauces.

Asher snipped the dead leaves, made sure there were still ladybugs around—he knew them to be a predator of aphids and other small parasitic bugs—and made sure that none of the buds or blooms were becoming diseased.

When Asher was done tending the Romas, he sat and laid his head on his arm on the side of the tomato box. He stared at the plants, too tired to get up after a long day and stomach full of J.J.'s dinner. He thought about times past when he tended this garden with his brother... with his mother. He thought about the things she had taught him about being kind to nature. Asher remembered the song with the nonsense lyrics again—Arrirang, Arrirang, Arrariyo...

*****

Asher hears voices.

"The Painting Man is getting closer… the boss is checkin' things out… couple of ants have gone missing…"

He cannot see where the voices are coming from. He could not see anything.

Am I dreaming? Where am I? This doesn't feel like a dream. Where is the garden? I'm nowhere…

Now Asher sees his tomato plants again, but this time they have tomatoes. NO!! These are not his tomatoes. These tomatoes, the ones he sees now before his face, are in a bowl. He's on a table in a small candlelit room—not his deck! Asher sits up quickly and finds himself in the middle of a spread of sweet and savory-smelling colorful dishes of food and… bugs? He's surrounded by bugs eating dinner?!

Eating him!!! Not a dream—a nightmare!

No, not eating him. The bugs are in as much shock to see him as he is to see them.

A bug, maybe a ladybug except for the beard and sort of human face with its two human eyes and almost human mouth is the first to make a sound. "You're him! You're the boy!"

"I'm who?"

"You're the boy. Uh-oh Halfwing. The boy ain't that smart. What does that mean?" The ladybug-man is speaking to a moth. A moth?

"Hush up, Spots. He's confused, he doesn't know where he is." This is an old moth by the sound of her raspy voice and wrinkles. Wrinkles? Moths have an exo-skeleton, they shouldn't have wrinkles. But this one does. "Child, you're safe here. You may not know it, but we are friends of yours."

Asher is struggling to comprehend this. "You're friends? I don't know you. You're not friends."

The aged moth speaks again to him from her chair at the head of the table. "Yes, Asher, we are your friends."

She knows my name! They know my name!

Asher noticed now that there is also an earthworm, only with arms and a face. And a spider as well, a pretty spider. *Huh? How can a spider be pretty?*

He feels a hand gently rest on top of his own and immediately feels calm—it is the hand of the moth. "Asher, we are friends, I promise." And he believes her. "We've known about you as long as we've known ourselves."

"Who are you?" Asher now notices he is sitting in a bowl of mashed potatoes and his foot is in a salad.

The moth begins to speak but Asher cannot hear her. He feels as if he is spinning and twirling down a whirlpool of twisting space. A rumbling sound is throwing him, or maybe his mind, around in this whirlpool of space—whirlpool of nothing. The rumbling keeps coming at him, but it is familiar somehow. *Where did the table of food and the bugs go? Where is the pretty spider and the moth? The comforting moth.* What is this rumbling sound that is grabbing and pulling him through the whirlpool? Why is it familiar? Is the rumble saying his name?

"Asher, wake up. Let me take you to bed." Ray is speaking in a low and soft voice right into Asher's ear. He lifts his son up from the planter box and his son's eyes finally open.

"Dad. Dad?" Asher calls as he lays his head on his father's shoulder and wraps his arms around his father's neck. Asher is almost too big and heavy for this now, but Ray couldn't help

Derek Rey

himself.

"Yes, son?"

"I think that malt gave me weird dreams. You might have weird dreams tonight too."

"Maybe so, son. I don't remember my dreams as well these days as I used to when I was a little boy. What were you dreaming about?"

"Bugs."

"I guess that is a pretty weird dream. I hope that if I have strange dreams tonight that I get to remember them tomorrow when I wake up."

"If I have more dreams tonight, I'll tell you about them."

Ray lays Asher down in his bed and kisses his forehead and his cheek.

"I love you Dad, good night."

"Good night." Ray exits Asher's room and leaves the door open just a crack.

Asher looks over to his alarm clock that sits on his windowsill. 09:55

Lucie might still be awake. He reaches up to the corner of his windowsill past the alarm clock to the funnel. "Lucie!"

"What? I'm reading." He heard Lucie's response from the funnel.

"Nothing. Just seeing if you were awake. I had a weird dream."

"What was it about?"

"Bugs."

"Yeah, that's weird."

"Uh-huh. And it seemed like they knew me, but I didn't know them. And they had faces and they were as big as me. Bigger actually, they were like grown up people."

"Still weird."

"Uh-huh. And it felt weird too. Like I traveled through outer space or a wormhole to get there and then I went through the wormhole or something like that to get back before I could wake up."

"You read too much science fiction. Read my Black Beauty books or Nancy Drew, those are fun."

Asher pauses, not knowing how to respond. He isn't sure, but he doesn't think the dream has anything to do with the kinds of books he reads. "I'm going back to sleep. I'll see you tomorrow, okay?"

"Night."

"Night."

Alta Neighbors sits up in her chair with a start. *The barrier has been broken. It has started.* She knows that she needs to speak to Asher very soon. Things are going to get dangerous and she needs to keep Asher safe. So much depends on it.

Derek Rey

Day 2 – A Boy and His Home

The Offer

The window in Asher's room faced north so that the morning sun came in and shone at an angle on his far wall. It was enough light that Asher felt the need to wake. He stretched. He yawned and smelled bacon cooking. Dad was making breakfast and it was the first official full day of summer break; there would probably be waffles too—maybe with Mr. Harper's berries and some whipped cream.

Asher stretched again then scooted out of bed and started toward the living room. As he approached his door he heard talking coming from somewhere in his apartment. He recognized the voices to be his father and Mr. Harper. He glanced over at his alarm clock—07:41—this was too early for Mr. Harper to be here. He stepped out of his room and could tell that the tone of the conversation that was taking place was serious. Asher stood and listened, aware they did not know he could hear them speaking.

"Yes—yes, I was surprised too, Ray. Like I said, we weren't advertising anything like that." Mr. Harper's intense voice, though quiet, was still completely audible where Asher stood.

"So, how far into things are you?" The sound of his father's voice was filled with angst over whatever this subject was.

"We've seen some preliminary paperwork and the offer is

greater than the market value. It's something that Anne and I *must* consider; it would be foolish not to." Mr. Harper sounded as if this was a bad thing as much as it seemed to be a good thing.

"I won't ask how much but based on what you've told me this morning, I guess it must be a lot. I understand." Asher knew that despite what his father just said, his father did not understand, or could not understand. "How long do you and Anne have to accept or deny the offer?"

"Breitel hasn't given us a timeline, but it's clear that he wants this building as soon as he can get it, something about starting construction on something new before the summer is over."

What?! What did Mr. Harper mean by 'this building…'? He couldn't be talking about the apartments and their home… and the market, and J.J.'s…

"What does J.J. say about this?"

"I'm not sure. He actually owns the space that his restaurant occupies so his will be a separate sale."

What could Mr. Harper mean by all of this? 'Sale?' The word hit Asher in the gut, hard. Thoughts of his home, the only home he knows, spun wildly in his mind. His best friend in the entire world was only feet away from his home. What about his garden? The one that really belongs to his mother but in his own way, he takes care of it for her now. He couldn't let his mother's garden be given away to someone else.

"Frank, tell me. Do you think you'll be selling the building or not? This is something that affects Asher and I more than it does you. We're still recovering from last summer and this home is one of the few comforts that is helping us to heal."

"I know, I know Ray. That's why this has been difficult for Anne and myself." Mr. Harper's voice was filled with guilt.

"I don't mean to make this harder on you, but I need to know because Asher isn't ready for something like this."

Asher's eyes were filling with tears and his nose began to run. He couldn't think anymore, his breathing sputtered and caught in his throat. He ran out from his hiding place and screamed the only thing that his broken thinking could put together: "NO! You can't! Not my mom's garden! You can't give away my mom's garden! It's not yours!"

Ray came quickly and picked Asher up, buried his son's head into his chest and kissed the top of his head and spoke soothingly to him. "No son, we don't know if anything like that is going to happen." Asher's sobs were muffled by Ray's chest and shirt.

Frank knew to give Ray and his son this moment. He came this early to prevent Asher from hearing about this prematurely and he felt terrible that Asher woke and heard it anyway. "I'll go now Ray, I don't know if we're going to sell, but I promise you'll be the first to know." Frank Harper turned and left the two alone.

Ray laid his cheek on the top of his son's head. "Asher, it'll work out. Whatever happens, you and I will be together and that's all that matters."

Asher pushed away from his father. "NO! It's not all that matters! This is still Mom's and Simon's house. That's still Mom's garden." Asher was screaming at his father, something he never did, but he couldn't help himself.

"Son, I promise you that I'll keep things okay for us. We'll be alright."

Asher didn't know what to do. "No. No no no no no no…" He was shaking his head and sobbing. He turned around and ran back into his room. Slamming the door behind him, he fell onto his bed and buried his face into his blanket and pillow. He felt as if his mother was dying all over again and he was losing his brother for a second time. He didn't hear the door open, but he felt his father's hands on his shoulder and head. He felt his father lay his head next to his own. Asher still couldn't say or do anything except cry with his eyes shut tight, but he did hear his father sniffling. He felt his father's body next to his own; it shook with its own sadness. The two of them lay there for a long time. Though his tears did not stop, Asher quieted. Ray did not move. He held his son as closely as he possibly could, as if he would never let go, as if they could, over time, grow into one being—if such a thing could exist.

Minutes passed, though they felt like hours. Ray finally sat up and told his son that he was going to finish cooking breakfast and that it would be waiting for him when he came out.

*****

Later that morning after Asher had eaten a silent breakfast with his father, showered, and dressed, he went to his funnel-phone and called to Lucie. "Hey Lucie, can you hear me?"

A few seconds went by and then he heard her. "Yeah. What time is it?" She was obviously just waking up.

"It's 10:07. You're not up yet?"

"No, umm… yes, you woke me up. I fell asleep reading. Eww... I drooled all over my book!"

Asher would normally have made fun of her, first for drooling and second for telling him when she didn't have to, but he had business on his mind. "Get yourself up and dressed and meet me at the rocks."

"I'll need to shower first."

"Just hurry, I need to talk to you. It's really, really important."

"What is it? Are we going to do something? Did something happen?" She was awake now, and excited. Asher usually wasn't this eager about things; he normally was more cool and collected. Lucie thought this had to be big, whatever it was.

"Lucie, just get ready and meet me at the rocks as soon as you can. Okay?" Asher got up from his bed and let the funnel go. As he ran out of his room, he grabbed his backpack and heard Lucie say something more but ignored it. He stopped by the kitchen, grabbed a thermos and filled it with juice, and made a couple of ham and cheese sandwiches, taking no time to do anything extra. He wanted to get to the rocks and talk to Lucie, now.

Derek Rey

Bad News at The Rocks

Lucie jumped out of bed, grabbed some clothes, and ran to the bathroom, throwing her clothes for the day on the bathroom counter as she started her shower. A while later she was on her way out of her home, hair wet, Pop-Tarts in hand with her father calling after her. "Sorry Dad, I gotta go meet Asher at the rocks; he's got something planned for today." And with that, she was gone, not seeing the drawn looks of worry on her parents' faces. They indeed had important things to talk to her about. Frank and Anne worried that hearing the news from Asher would put things out of their control, but they couldn't catch her in time as she ran out the door.

A minute later she was at the rocks. Asher was pacing. He almost seemed nervous. "What's up Asher?"

Asher stopped his pacing and looked Lucie straight in the eyes. "Umm… did you talk to your parents this morning?"

"No." Then Lucie was really curious, Asher didn't play games like this with her parents as pawns.

Asher started pacing again, obviously thinking. He stopped and looked at her once again. "Your mom and dad are going to sell the building."

Lucie was halted by this. "Your joking!! What's really going on?" Lucie knew better, she knew when Asher was faking her out and she knew when he spoke the truth. This was him speaking the truth, but she wanted to be wrong, wanted him to be lying.

"I'm not kidding! I heard your dad tell my dad this morning." There was silence for a short moment. Lucie understood implicitly what this meant to Asher. The garden, Simon... this home was his anchor, his roots to maintain hope that his brother would get better and his feelings would heal from losing his mother. She didn't know this in a conscious, clinical way, but in the way that best friends always just knew.

Lucie spoke up finally, "What do we do?"

"I'm not sure yet, I can't come up with anything. I've been trying but I can't." Asher needed his friend right now to help him think straight and she knew it—Asher always had answers, she just had to ask the right questions.

"What did you hear my dad say to yours?"

Asher stopped pacing at this question; his eyes became intense, looking at nothing really, but thinking back to the morning instead. "Your dad was saying that he and your mom weren't trying to sell the building. That they got an offer 'from out of nowhere.' That he'd seen some papers with a huge offer and that the people offering want to do it quickly so they can tear the building down and start to build something else before summer was over."

"Did you see the papers too?"

"No. But that's it! Your dad didn't have the papers, so they must be in your home somewhere!"

"So? How's that going to help us?" Lucie had no idea what to do with information that would be on business papers, but she thought that Asher might know.

"First, we need to figure out who the offer is from and we can ask Mrs. Neighbors for some help. I don't think she would want to leave here either."

Lucie agreed, "She couldn't find anyone like you and your dad and my family to help her every day anywhere else."

Asher still didn't quite know what they were going to do, but he knew where to start. Asher pulled the thermos of juice and sandwiches out of his backpack and shared with Lucie. He also pulled out a notebook and pencil. They spoke about going to the library to look up information about whoever was trying to buy the building, they discussed who else might be able to help— maybe K.K., maybe Jenny Neighbors—but for sure Mrs. Neighbors would help. Then they talked about what their lives might be like if they couldn't stop it. Where would they move? It would certainly be far apart from each other because the Harper's would have quite a bit of money and Asher and his father would still be struggling. Maybe Lucie would end up in the West Hills and Asher would move out to Clackamas or Gresham where homes weren't so expensive. That's far enough apart that they might as well move to different states from each other.

"Lucie, we have to stop them from selling."

"I know. Okay, I'll go and find the papers and see if I can get any good information from it."

"Make a copy in your Dad's office on the Xerox."

"I will."

Asher knew that Lucie's parents would know that he told her before they had a chance to speak to her. "Lucie, we have to come up with a story about what we talked about."

"What do you mean?" Lucie didn't see a need.

"Your parents will know I told you about all of this because your dad knows that I know."

Lucie got it now, "That's why my parents wanted to talk to me before I left."

"Yeah. Here's what you do…" And Asher explained the plan.

88

The Papers and a Name

Asher walked back into his home and found his father typing away at the far end of the bar. He went up to his dad and climbed up into his lap. Asher was getting pretty big these days for doing something like this, but his dad never stopped him.

"You okay, kiddo?" Ray said this to his son, whose head was on his shoulder.

"No."

"Do you need anything?"

"No."

"Are ya sure?"

"No."

"Can you say anything besides 'No'?"

"Maybe."

"Okay." Ray sat with Asher on his lap for another moment. Eventually Asher slid down. "Do you feel better?"

"Yeah." Asher stood facing his father now. "I'll be alright Dad. I know you'll make everything okay, even if we can't stay here. I'm just really sad about the garden."

"Do you want to tell me about it?"

"Not really. But... Mom, when we made this garden, said that it was my job and Simon's job to keep it going. She gave me the book about gardening on a deck and she showed Simon everything he needed to do every day. It was like 'our thing.' Now I'm the only one left to take care of it for Mom so I have to protect it, but I can't. I take care of it for her every day."

"Asher, we can take the planter boxes with us whereever we move to."

"I know Dad, but it was there that Mom, Simon and I put it all together. It feels like I'm with Mom still when I'm out there."

Ray was at a loss now, he came up with the best thing he could think of, "Well, maybe the Harper's won't sell. Mr. Harper hasn't made a decision yet."

"I think he has Dad." Asher didn't want to argue with his father, so he then said, "But maybe you're right. I think I'm going to go and read."

Ray patted his son's shoulder. "I've gotta finish this and get it to the paper, I think I'll do it at the office. Call me if you need anything."

"Okay, I will."

Asher walked back to his bedroom and his father pulled the paper out of his typewriter and headed out the door. He had meant every word of the conversation he had just had with his father, but he had also accomplished exactly what he had set out to do—get his father to give him some space and leave him alone.

Asher grabbed the funnel-phone, "Lucie?"

"I can't get to the papers yet," her voice rang out the of the funnel.

"That's alright, we should give my dad a little while to get all the way to the office, just to be sure he isn't going to come back for anything he might have forgotten. How well did it go?"

"Perfectly!!! They did exactly what you said. After I came in pretending to cry and be mad at them, which wasn't hard because I AM mad at them, my dad went out to work in the market and my mom started cleaning. She's organizing in the office right now, that's why I can't get to the papers but after that she'll probably go to the kitchen next and clean everything 'cause that's what she always does when we're fighting so I think that I can get into the office pretty soon."

"Let me know when you get the papers. I'll be waiting here by the funnel."

*****

Spots was standing beside Halfwing and Legs. He said to the other two, "I don't understand what happened in there last night. How did the Boy appear like that then disappear? How'd you know his name Halfwing?"

Halfwing did her moth-version of a shrug, wings slightly raising and dropping, "I don't know, Spots. Something big must be happening, I can feel it inside. I just saw him, and I knew it, as if I heard someone else's thoughts for a moment and they knew his name."

Legs spoke up, "You realize this means that the Painting Man probably knows that something's brewing up too. We need to be ready."

Halfwing showed her worry, "The Boss and Digger will bring us some news, maybe then we can start to find some answers."

Spots said, "I hope so, things are gettin' weird around here. First, Digger shows up, an' then the Boy an' also what happened to the ants… I don't like it. I'll be honest with ya two, I'm pretty scared right now."

*****

Asher heard Lucie's voice through the funnel, "I found them, I made a copy."

"Great!! Ask your mom if you can come up and help me with the garden for a while. She never says 'no' to that."

"Okay, but Asher, you're not going to like what I have to show you."

What Does Contingent Mean?

Lucie knocked on Asher's front door and he let her in. They went straight for the couch and coffee table, which Asher had already cleared off. Lucie spread out all the papers, fifteen in all. With the pages laid before them, they were lost; everywhere they looked they could hardly understand anything. The two children could pick out words here and there, but, putting them in the order they were in, made extraordinarily little sense. Lucie had spent more time with it earlier and found all the information she herself could understand and she showed it to Asher.

"A man named Breitel wants to buy this building, so he can demolish it and build an investment property."

"Does it say what kind of investment property?" Asher asked.

"No, that's all it says. At least I think that's all it says." She paused for a moment and then said pleadingly, "But look at this Asher, look how much he wants to pay my parents." She sat back on the couch with her arms crossed.

Asher noticed her posture and the expression on her face told him just how upset she really was. He turned and looked at what she pointed to and said, "Seven million dollars!!! There's no way your parents can say 'no' to this, Lucie."

"I know. You'd think I'd be happier; I mean… we're going to be rich—really rich."

"Yeah, your folks could buy ten houses in the West Hills and still have so much left over." He said this and then turned his head down, looking at that number, that insurmountable number.

Neither Asher nor Lucie knew what to do. They had hoped that a simple argument and some begging and pleading would do the trick to knock this silly offer out of Lucie's parents' minds, but now they know better. This was an *adults-only* decision, and it was obvious what that decision would be.

Asher noticed something in the papers that seemed important. "Hey Lucie, there's a section that reads: 'The completion of the sale of said property is contingent upon simultaneous sale of the property owned by J.J.'s Diner, LLC with all final agreements made with the parties of Anton Breitel, buyer, Frank and Anne Harper, seller, and J.J.'s Diner LLC, seller, present in person.' Maybe J.J. isn't going to sell; he makes a lot of money from the diner."

"What does 'contingent' mean?" She was perplexed but she understood that it must be important.

Asher was so excited he almost yelled when he said, "It means that J.J. has to sell too or the sale for your parents' property won't go through… and everything stays the same!"

"J.J. won't sell, he loves that diner."

"I know, but we need to know for sure."

Lucie didn't say anything else, she just jumped up and over the coffee table and ran out the door. Asher followed, knowing she was going to go and ask K.K. if she thought that J.J. would sell. Neither of them would ever try talking to J.J. about something like this; he'd simply tell them it was none of their business and then make them mop up his kitchen for wasting his time. They ran out the door, down the stairs, out to the sidewalk, and around the corner to a side door of the diner. They quietly opened the side door, knowing it was unlocked and hoping that J.J. was not right there. They peeked in and saw K.K. cutting some vegetables on a prep counter.

Lucie called in a loud whisper, "K.K., come here."

J.J. yelled out from somewhere unseen, "WHAT?! What'd ya say Katherine Kelly?!"

K.K. turned to respond to her father and that's when she saw Asher and Lucie at the door, both a little terrified from hearing J.J.'s voice. She covered for them, "Sorry Dad, I just coughed. I'm going to step outside for a minute, so I don't cough all over the kitchen, okay?"

"Hurry it up! I don't want you gettin' behind. You got the prep done yet?" He asked the last question in a tone that made both Asher and Lucie shrink away.

"Dad, I know how to do my job! Leave me alone, I know the kitchen as well as you do!" And J.J. started to say something more but K.K. closed the door on him, which seriously impressed the two intimidated children.

Lucie spoke up with big, round, deer-in-headlights eyes, "What's J.J. going to do to you when you go back in?"

"Nothing. He knows I'm right; that's just how he is and as long as I do my job well, he's never really mad at all, just a bit noisy. To what do I owe the pleasure? It's been a while since I've seen your heads pop in our side door like that."

Lucie again started in, "Umm… Umm…."

Asher stepped in, "The Harpers got an offer to…"

Lucie interrupted Asher now in her machine-gun quick delivery, "… to sell our house and the produce market and the apartment where Asher and Mrs. N. live and even Bruno's… I mean… EVERYTHING…but they can't sell unless J.J.'s Diner LLC… er… I mean J.J. sells the diner too but we don't think that

J.J. will sell because he loves this place too much and he'll probably give it to you when he retires so he won't want to give it to someone else I mean I think that anyway 'cause Asher and I didn't talk about that part so I don't know if he thinks that too but I know he thinks that J.J. won't sell 'cause that's what he said earlier and since my parents can't sell unless J.J. sells we came to ask you FOR SURE if J.J. is going to sell or not and we think he won't. Please, please, please, please..." she was jumping up and down with her hands clasped under her chin for this last part.

K.K. looked at Lucie somewhat bewildered, "What?!"

Lucie shot back, "Is your dad going to sell the diner?"

K.K. leaned against the door, sighed, and looked out into the Park Blocks for the answers, "Well kids, let me talk to you like you're grown-ups."

They nodded in unison.

"Lucie, Asher, my dad loves this place because we get to do it together, but when I finish culinary school, I have to go wherever I get the best job. We talked about it and he's decided that the best thing to do is sell."

The two children understood exactly what K.K. was trying to tell them. The sale is a done deal. K.K. grabbed them and held them in her arms like they were family, said that she was sorry, and then went back in to finish her prep.

Asher and Lucie decided to go back and gather up the papers and talk about it at the rocks. They thought that maybe they might handle this better or think better at the rocks. So off they went and were soon sitting on the ground, leaning up against the massive stone that lay at the center of Peace Chant, protected on all sides by stone guardians. And there they sat, long enough for the sun to move from behind one tree to another, not knowing what to do next. After a while, the talk was no longer of the situation at hand, but instead it was of other things, the kind of things that twelve-year olds usually talk about like the Blazers in the playoffs, He-Man versus anyone from the Justice League, and so on and so forth. This kind of talk didn't hurt like when they were coming to terms with their situation, feeling small and childish and helpless. They even talked about a fort they were planning on building on the roof of the produce market until they remembered that they probably wouldn't be able to. Thoroughly defeated, they got up and each went to their respective homes. Lucie needed to help her mother make dinner as she did most nights and Asher needed to clear his mind; he thought reading some Asimov would help with that.

The Other Garden

Asher was at the top of the stairs getting ready to turn left toward his apartment as he said "hello" to Mrs. Neighbors. As he grabbed the door handle to his apartment, he heard her give a raspy cough.

"Come here son, come visit with me for a little bit."

Asher was not in the mood. All he really wanted to do was go and take his mind off his problems, but Asher was raised to respect the people in his life who took care of him, and that included Mrs. Neighbors. He walked into her apartment and said "hi" and suddenly felt awkward for saying "hello" and then saying "hi" right afterward.

"Hello again darling. Come sit by me; you look as if you feel like a Macy's parade balloon deflated and fell crashing to the ground."

Asher thought about that image and then said "Yep, I think you got it Mrs. N. That's just about how I feel."

"It doesn't have anything to do with a recent revelation regarding our precarious living arrangements, does it?"

"Mrs. N., I don't like this. This is our home. I don't want to leave it." Asher wanted to say more but he stopped himself for fear of his trembling chin and a stubborn lump in his throat completely taking over his power of speech and turning him into a blubbering mass of tears and snot. He turned his head away from Mrs. Neighbors and clenched his jaw to keep control.

Mrs. Neighbors sat conflicted. She was unsure of how exactly to help this boy. This boy that was so fragile, yet so much more powerful than he could have imagined. She grasped his head with both hands and turned him toward her and stared deeply into his eyes, forcing him to keep her gaze. "Son. You will not have to move. You will not have to leave your home and uproot your mother's garden. Do you understand me?"

"Yes, I will. You will too Mrs. N. And so will Lucie. We saw how much Breitel is offering her parents for the building and K.K. already told us that her dad was going to accept his offer from Breitel too. There's nothing I can do, or Lucie, or you."

"That's where you're wrong son. You have to be wrong because you must keep that garden where it is, and you must continue to care for it."

"Huh? What are you talking about Mrs. N.?"

She continued to hold his face to hers like a stern, powerful, and loving grandmother. "Asher, I have some things to share with you… to show you. Come with me." She grasped Asher's shoulder to help lift herself up then let him guide her across the hall and into his apartment. She walked him straight to the glass door to the garden. "There son. That is what I have to show you."

"Umm… Mrs. N. I still don't understand. I already knew I had a garden there." Asher said this hoping not to sound flippant or disrespectful.

"Son… Asher… take me out to your garden."

He slowly nodded and did as was asked of him, opening the door, and holding her hand as they walked onto the deck. Mrs. Neighbors spoke, "Look around son. Look carefully."

Asher looked. Everything looked the same as it had for the last year except that the plants were a little fuller now. Two planter boxes of herbs, Italian parsley, thyme, oregano, and some mint. There were two planter boxes of tomatoes, one with the San Marzano variety and the other with cherry and beefsteak. A box of onions and garlic ran along the edge so that the wind would blow the smell away from the door. He looked at the box of green beans and finally two boxes of blueberries in the corner, where sunlight would fall for the greatest number of hours. They stood there for a moment and Asher finally said, "Mrs. N., I still don't get it. I'm the one who told you I didn't want to leave this garden or this home. What are you trying to tell me?"

"Son, let's sit," and with that Asher grabbed a bucket for Mrs. Neighbors and he sat right on the floor of the deck. "Look around again Asher. Now, I want you to face me and close your eyes but imagine yourself still in this garden." He did as she asked. "Now imagine yourself in this garden but with nothing else around, no building here, no glass door, no Park Blocks across the street, no sidewalk and road below… just you and the plants." She stroked his hair behind his ears then softly laid her hands on his shoulders. "Keep imagining yourself and all these plants and wipe everything else away from your mind. Just you and the tomatoes, the blueberries, the beans…"

Asher imagined all this and heard Mrs. Neighbors' voice grow quiet and distant and then he and the plants were swirling around the same dreamlike whirlpool that he had felt once before. All around him it became dark and light at the same time, and then he was again in his garden, but it was not the same. It was larger. Instead of planter boxes, he saw long rows in the ground with dozens of plants. He saw small fields, enough to feed a village. All this was surrounded by tall fir trees and maples and beechwoods. Bugs were tending the plants and … BUGS!! Big bugs, with tools.

Ants mostly, but also a spider and in front of him, facing away, was a group of three—a ladybug, a spider, and a moth.

Asher was confounded. He was most confused by the fact that he was not scared. Maybe it was because he recognized these person-sized bugs as the same that were in his dream the previous night. No, that wasn't it… he wasn't afraid because he felt like he knew this place, like he belonged here. And in this small moment of realization the moth turned and saw him.

"Asher! Stay there! It's okay, we are friends." And then the spider and the ladybug turned and were elated at the sight of him. He didn't know why they were so happy, but he knew that these were long-lost friends, or something of the sort. He stood still, not sure if he was really where he was, and watched the bugs walk… crawl… whatever it was… toward him. The spider arrived first and shook his hand. What? *This spider has a hand?* Then the ladybug did the same but a bit more gregariously. And finally, the moth, which looked quite old and worn with her one-third wing and wrinkled face, was in front of him and she grabbed him with both hands and hugged him closely and wrapped her wings around him. She pulled away and said "I am Halfwing, for obvious reasons; this is Spots, and this is Legs. We are so very pleased to have you here in the Garden."

"Thank you." Asher spoke his first two words this trip in this new world. He didn't know what to say after that. This couldn't be real; it must be some kind of hypnotic trick that Mrs. N. was pulling to cheer Asher up.

"Is that all you got to say?" said Spots, "Oh my, Halfwing, I think there's somethin' wrong with him."

"There's nothing wrong with me." Asher knew now that this was completely real. He was having a conversation with a moth, a spider, and a ladybug who somehow knew who he was. "What is this place?"

Spots laughed and said, "It's where we live; it's the garden." He patted Asher's shoulder, which almost sent him falling to the ground. "Oops, sorry 'bout that. I forget that I can do that to the little ones." Asher really was considerably smaller than the three bugs in front of him.

"Uhh... I don't understand why I'm here, or what this place is. Or even how it can be... just be." Asher was almost angry at not being able to understand. He felt a finger go down the side of his head and he saw that Halfwing was pushing his hair behind his ear and this calmed him immediately; she then held his cheek in her hand. Something felt very comforting about the way she did this.

"Listen to me, child. We really don't know the answers to your questions either. But what we do know is that we ARE here, we live here, and this is our home. We are a family in this place. We don't really know how we got here."

Asher cocked his head to the side, "But wouldn't you have come here from somewhere else or been born here and that would be how you got here?"

Legs said in a very matter-of-fact tone, "That's the thing, we don't remember those things happening. We only remember just being here just as we are today."

Asher was beginning to understand. This must be some sort of parallel universe like Stephen Hawking talks about; it seemed too real to be anything other than that, but it also seemed impossible.

Halfwing went on to explain more. "We are glad that you've found your way here. You are the source of us."

"What do you mean?"

"This place comes from you, it exists because you exist," she said.

"Okay, let's say I believe you; how do you know that it exists because I exist?"

"I've just known. I could always see you." Halfwing was speaking the truth, he could tell. "The others can't and I'm not sure why. But when our plants grow, I know it's from you, when Digger arrived, he came here because you put him here."

"Who is Digger?" Asher asked wondering just how many people… er, bugs, lived in this place.

"He's a worm, new to this place but very much a part of our family already" she said.

At this, Asher thought of the worm he placed in the tomato box the other day and it began to fit together in his mind, although he still had a difficult time believing this. "Where is Digger? How's he doing? When I put him in the tomato box, he was almost dead."

Spots said, "He's fine now, but he was a wreck when he got here. I almost killed him but Halfwing stopped me. He was mostly just thirsty when he came up from the ground."

"Yeah, he was almost dried out when I put him in the box, thirsty makes sense." Asher more and more believed that this was real. He couldn't understand it, but he also couldn't argue with the realness of everything around him.

"Digger is with the Boss right now" said Halfwing "they're drawing up a plan to go and save one of our friends from the Painting Man."

"Who is the Painting Man?"

Legs said, "A bad, bad man, there's no other way to put it."

"Is he some kind of bug too?"

"No, he's a man like you but a lot bigger."

Halfwing added, "He's why we are so glad to see you. We need your help because the Painting Man is taking more territory. His place is far enough away that he leaves us alone, but he has slaves and soldiers who cut down the trees around his walls and they are moving toward us. A few of the ants died after running into them and one has been taken prisoner."

"What can I do? I don't even know how I made this place to begin with."

Halfwing began to speak but before she completed her first word everything went black and Asher felt the twirling, swirling, nothingness and then he was looking straight into Mrs. Neighbor's eyes, once again standing in his own garden on his deck.

"You're back! Good, your father is coming up the stairs, I just saw him come up the sidewalk and into the door down below."

Asher was immobilized with shock and confusion. He remembered everything that had just happened, but his sense of disbelief was renewed by his return to the real world.

"Son! Get with it, your father just entered the apartment, we need to look like everything is normal. Now snip some oregano." She handed him the shears. He didn't know where they had come from but apparently Mrs. N. was prepared.

"Hi, kiddo. Whatcha doin' out here?" Ray Jakes said to his son, who was now dutifully snipping oregano.

"Oh, umm, Mrs. N. and I were going to have some spaghetti." Spaghetti was the first thing he thought of since Lucie had it just the night before.

"Yes son," she said to Ray, "we weren't sure if you were going to be late home with a deadline tonight."

"Nope, finished a couple of hours ago, I was with Simon then came home to take you two to J.J.'s. I didn't call because I thought Asher and Lucie would be out saving the world somewhere in the Park Blocks. J.J.'s cooking meatloaf and strawberry rhubarb pie tonight."

Mrs. Neighbors said, "That sounds delicious son, I'll save these cuttings for something tomorrow, perhaps a summer soup for lunch." This saved her and Asher since they really weren't planning on spaghetti or anything else for that matter.

Ray said, "Let's go then, before it gets too busy in the diner."

"Okay Dad." Asher jumped up and ran to his bedroom to put on a clean change of clothes. He had let himself get quite grubby in the park earlier that day and knew that J.J. would give him a death stare for showing up in his diner "looking like Pig-Pen."

As he changed, Asher could not get the experience in the other garden out of his mind, the one with the human sized bugs that had hands and this Painting Man they kept talking about and how it seemed so familiar even though he'd never seen it before. He couldn't get it out of his mind that Halfwing claimed that it was all his own creation. Asher was quiet at dinner, for the same reason. Luckily, Mrs. Neighbors was there to cover for his inattentive behavior.

After dinner, as they all went back upstairs to their respective homes, Mrs. Neighbors gave Asher a knowing grasp of the shoulder and told him to have a good night's sleep and that everything would be alright. Ray asked her if she needed anything. She responded with, "A grown man needs his sleep too, son. Get to bed."

"Yes ma'am."

Later in his room, Asher called to Lucie through the funnel-phone, "Lucie, are you there?"

"Yeah, I can't sleep. I've just been thinking about this place. I don't want to move away from here, Asher." Asher could tell that she had been crying, her voice was a little higher than normal and a little strained. He didn't say anything because he knew that she would be self-conscious about crying; she always tried to be tough and not cry.

"Hey Lucie, I had that dream again about the big bugs." He hoped to get her mind off of the difficult matters, but he also wanted to tell her about what had *really* happened to him earlier that evening with Mrs. N. on the deck.

"Yeah? Did they eat you this time?" As she said this, Asher could almost hear her laugh a little.

"No! They were gardening and talking to me." He wanted to say more, but he couldn't bring himself to do it, not really sure if he, himself, really believed it. "That's it, then I woke up."

"Then go back to sleep, I need to sleep too." Asher heard the clink of the funnel hitting Lucie's wall, then he heard the whoosh of the hose as she grabbed it again and said, "Hey Asher?"

"Yeah."

"When I woke up this morning, I was so excited for summer to begin. I was happy, and I couldn't wait for what we were going to do today."

"Yeah, me too."

"But then... you know... things changed."

"Yeah." Asher's gut tightened.

"When we wake up tomorrow, I'm not going to be excited."

"Me either."

"I'm not really excited for the summer anymore."

"Me either."

"Goodnight."

Clink

"Good night Lucie."

Clink

*****

Far away from the garden tended by bugs, beyond many stands of trees, in a field that once was forest, loomed a tall wall made of cut trees. This wall extended for several hundred yards and at the top of the wall, the trees had been carved to sharp points. Torches lined the top of the wall at twenty-foot intervals. Behind the wall was a compound, a fortress made of log and stone, surrounded on all sides by similar walls. The fortress comprised a dozen large structures of the same materials, built to withstand all except maybe the worst kind of fire that could never reach inside the walls. Of these dozen buildings, one stood taller and larger than all the rest and it was here that the Painting Man had his throne, carved from the trunk of one single fir tree that had a circumference measured in yards and a height that could only be guessed.

The Painting Man sat on his throne this night, his eyes dark slits and his lips slightly parted to reveal his gritted teeth. He spoke to a group of six soldiers, wood-eating grubs: "There is a worm within these walls. He has gotten past the lot of you. What do you say to this?"

The shortest but stoutest of these armored grubs apologized, "We don't know how it happened, we've been looking for him these last few hours since you first sensed him."

Spit and hatred flew from the mouth of the now-screaming despot, "UNACCEPTABLE!!! You will find him and bring him to me tonight or I will take you all and do to you what I would otherwise do to him." To make his point, he lifted a hand in the direction of the grub standing farthest away. It rose a few feet, then as he threw his hand down, the grub shot downward as well. It splattered and was gone. "Go. Now!"

The frightened grubs left as quickly as they could, knowing that the Painting Man meant exactly what he said. Tonight would be their last night unless they found the intruder.

Day 3 – A Boy and His Best Friend

Little White Lie

Asher woke up feeling like he hadn't had any sleep at all. He knew that he probably tossed and turned all night with bad dreams considering the type of day he had yesterday and was thankful that he could not remember those dreams.

It was Sunday, and that meant breakfast with Mrs. Neighbors and his father down at J.J.'s. He showered and dressed and found his father waiting for him in the living room with Mrs. Neighbors, which was not unusual on Sunday mornings, but he could tell that they had been talking about him by the way everything went silent as he came from the hallway. He ignored it. "Hi, Mrs. N. Dad, are we going to J.J.'s now?"

"Yep, come and help Mrs. Neighbors up and we'll get going." Ray got up and patted his son on the back as they passed each other, Asher to help Mrs. Neighbors and Ray to put away a column he was working on.

Mrs. Neighbors leaned in close to Asher's ear as she was getting up and quietly said, "I hope you remember everything from yesterday, son. You need to go back as soon as possible; there's a lot depending on you." And then she spoke more loudly, "Thank you son for helping this poor decrepit old woman up. Just look at me! I should be thrown out with the trash I'm so useless."

She winked at Asher and they both chuckled a little.

The three of them went down the stairs and were met at the door by the stray black-and-grey tabby who followed them to J.J.'s front door. "Dad, I think that stray might be hungry? Let's bring him some scraps when we leave."

"Sure, we can do that," Ray said.

They entered, sat, and had their normal Sunday breakfast. J.J. had made each of them French toast. They agreed, as they did every Sunday, that no one could ever make French toast like J.J. Once J.J. had said to them in his gruff tone, "The secret's in the bread, and I ain't tellin' you what kind of bread it is." He then turned and left before they could even respond. That was J.J.

They left and were met by the tabby who got a treat from Asher, a couple scraps of bacon. As they got to the door that led up to the apartments, Ray kept going straight, on his way to work. "One of the printers is sick; I have to help them out today." It was not uncommon for Ray to help out the other departments like that; with only one column and no other responsibilities the entire week, he often did extra work if his research and interviews for the columns were completed early. Asher and Mrs. Neighbors expected as much and went right upstairs.

As they got to the top of the stairs Asher said, "Mrs. N.... was that real yesterday?"

"Yes, son. It was."

"But how did you know?" he asked.

"Come sit with me and we'll talk about it. Besides, Jenny is coming over soon and she has some things to share with us."

They went in and sat down, Mrs. Neighbors in the avocado recliner and Asher on the floor against the wall within arm's reach of the chair. "You were going to tell me how you knew about it

Mrs. N."

"Yes. Well." She clapped her hands in front of her face and held them tight for a moment. "I don't know if I can explain it all that well, but I'll try. I can sense things Asher. I can feel your feelings, and other people's feelings as well, near or far, just by concentrating on it."

"You mean like you're psychic. I didn't think that was real," he said.

"Not exactly, I don't hear your thoughts; I can just tell what you're feeling. I can tell if people are nearby because I can feel them. Like right now, if I concentrate," and she did, "I can tell that Lucie is in her room, and both of her parents are in the living room; but Frank, Mr. Harper, is going out to the market right... now." Asher heard a faint thud, which was probably the door from their home to the market.

"So you can feel people," he said.

"Almost... I feel their feelings, and I get used to the feelings of the people I know so I can identify them that way. When you're angry, it's different from when your father's angry. When Lucie is excited, it's different from when you are excited. If strangers are walking on the sidewalk, I can feel their feelings as well—although I wouldn't know who they were—I can feel that they are there, on the sidewalk, outside our door."

"So Mrs. N., how did you know about the garden?" Asher asked.

"I can feel all of those people there. I don't quite know who they are, but there's something familiar about it, and it seems to be affected by you and your actions out there. When you put the worm in the dirt the other day, you made something happen. I felt it, it was immediate."

Asher got excited, "Yeah! You're right! There's a worm there now. He even has a name, Digger. There's a moth there named Halfwing who told me about him."

Mrs. Neighbors was astonished, "A worm and a moth? I thought that maybe there was some sort of place with people that we couldn't see that you could somehow be connected to. But... bugs?"

"Yeah, bugs. It's weird, but that's what they are. Bugs." Asher said this and it felt more real now. In fact, he would look back someday and recognize this very moment when he told Mrs. Neighbors about the bugs, as the moment that he truly believed and accepted that the garden with the bugs was real.

"Wow, I never imagined." She leaned toward Asher and began to tell more. "You know son, there are many places like your garden. I can feel them all over. Between here and Mrs. Lownsdale's market there are two more. Everywhere I go, I can feel them. But yours is different to me because this is the first time I've ever known a place like it to be connected to someone that I knew."

"What made you think I could go to it?"

"I honestly didn't know if you could go to it. But I thought you could at least feel it," she said.

"But why did you want me to feel or go to it?"

"Because there's another reason yours is different from all those other places I can feel. Your place began to have fear and pain where there used to only be happiness and content. All the other places I'm aware of never change; it's the same feelings, always. But yours has become more... alive." She stopped and pondered this idea.

"Mrs. Neighbors, there is a lot happening in the garden.

There's a bad guy, they call him the Painting Man. There's a friend of theirs that the Painting Man has kidnapped. They're trying to come up with a plan to save their friend and they say I have to help them, that they won't be able to do it without my help."

"That makes sense," she said, "I have also felt that something else, something new, is having an effect on your garden, and I didn't recognize it as coming from you. There must be someone else in your garden and he must be made to leave. If they can't do it alone, they'll need you to give them the strength to do it."

"But what if I don't know how to do what they need me to do?" Asher asked with a little bit of fear and uncertainty mixed together.

"I'm sorry son, it'll have to be another time. Jenny is coming, she's on the sidewalk in front of Harper's Market. Why don't you go and get Lucie, she should hear this as well." She put a hand behind Asher's shoulder to shove him along.

"Yes ma'am." Asher jumped up and ran to his room to call Lucie on the funnel-phone.

Soon, all four people were in Mrs. Neighbors' living room. Asher and Lucie were seated together on a loveseat across from Mrs. Neighbors, and Jenny Neighbors had pulled a chair from the kitchen.

Jenny Neighbors had straight, brown, shoulder-length hair and brown eyes. Asher noticed that she had a lot of make up on, but it looked nice. He had always thought that her face belonged on television and that it was appropriate that she had the job of a newscaster.

Jenny spoke now, "Asher, Lucie, I'm here because my grandmother asked me to help." She spoke with newscaster fortitude. "She explained to me on the phone Friday night that it looked like all of you were going to lose your homes."

"I don't want to leave any more than either of you two do. I also told her the name that you told me about, Lucie. Breitel," said Mrs. Neighbors.

Lucie asked, "But what can you do to stop it from happening, Jenny? Asher and I can't think of anything."

Asher nodded his agreement.

"Well, my grandmother knows that I know people who can find things out for us. Like a realtor that I speak to often about business moves in the area for many of the reports that I do, we've been friends since college. I called him Friday night and asked him to look into the sale of this building." She was smiling and the children noticed.

"And did he find out something useful?" Asher asked as Lucie sat anxiously next to him.

"He found the same name that you found, Lucie. He also found that Breitel has made more than a dozen land purchases in and around Portland; all of them are listed as investment properties in the paperwork."

"How did he find that all out?" Lucie asked.

"He has access to several offices because of his job, even on the weekends."

"What's Breitel doing with the investment properties he already owns?" Asher asked this time.

"That's the strange part. He isn't doing anything with them. There are no applications for construction with the city or county. There's nothing listed for resale. It looks like they're just sitting there. For investment purposes, they are essentially losing Breitel money right now; not very good investing if you ask me."

"I knew it," said Mrs. Neighbors, "I knew there was something wrong with that man. I think I saw him with Mr. Harper a few days ago and he seemed like he was hiding something, like he was not the kind of person I'd want to do business with."

Asher understood this to mean that Mrs. Neighbors *felt* something from Breitel that no one else would be able to sense. He looked right at Mrs. Neighbors and she gave him a slight, almost imperceptible nod when the others weren't looking that confirmed his thoughts.

"Where are these places? Maybe we can see something at one of them that might help us out?" Asher said.

"Like what?" Lucie asked.

"I don't know, but maybe he's doing something illegal in these buildings and then Jenny could do a story on this 'mysterious investor with shady dealings,'" Asher said in his estimation of TV news caster's voice, "and that might stop the sale of this building."

Mrs. Neighbors spoke up, "I don't know if I want you doing that, children. If he is doing anything illegal, it would be too dangerous for you."

"We can't tell my parents. They would be angry that we're interfering with their business; then they would want Jenny to stay out of it," Lucie said.

Jenny tried to reassure Lucie, "I don't want to offend your parents, Lucie, leave this to me for now. I can do a lot in the next couple of days and a sale like this takes a while; we have plenty of time to find out what we need to find out." Jenny stood up. "I have to go; I have an interview to do down by City Hall with a couple of the city council members."

"Thanks Jenny, my mom would be glad to know you're helping us," said Asher.

"Yes, I know. I'm doing this for her too. I would do anything for her; I was as close to her as I was my grandmother." She patted the two kids' heads, "I'll take care of things for you, I promise." She hugged her grandmother, kissed her on the cheek, and left.

After Jenny left, Mrs. Neighbors threw a file folder on her coffee table. "I want you kids to know that I told a little white lie earlier. Jenny would not agree to allowing you two to go and see these places, but I know you better. You are very capable, and you'll keep your distance from anyone."

They nodded, astonished at what they were hearing.

"You also will not enter any of those properties, do you understand?" she said sternly.

"Yes, ma'am," they both said.

"Here are the properties, she gave me a copy of the listings before you got back Asher." She slid the file to the two children and said, "You can go today, while businesses are closed, and traffic is slow. I'll cover for you and tell your parents you're shopping for me if they wonder, just let me know when you're going."

"Wow, thanks, Mrs. N. But what should we look for?" Asher asked.

"I don't have the slightest idea. Just take a look and see if anything is suspicious, but I repeat what I said earlier—stay safe." She again gave them that forbidding look. "I know you two are smart and you'll know how to stay out of trouble, just don't forget to actually stay out of it. You got it?"

"Yes Mrs. Neighbors," said Lucie with an excessively big grin.

"We understand Mrs. Neighbors," said Asher and he picked up the file and started across the hall to his own apartment. "We'll let you know what we find. Bye Mrs. N." Lucie followed Asher and waved goodbye to Mrs. Neighbors.

The two were across the hall now. Alta Neighbors sat alone, a little afraid. She could feel that the two children understood and were going to be smart and safe, but a little part of her was still afraid.

Derek Rey

The Boss

The table in Asher's living room was covered with the pages from the file. An old map of Portland that Asher owned was now marked with a route from location to location so that they could get to all the properties. "It's going to be hard to make it to all those places, Lucie." Asher shook his head with doubt.

Lucie felt defeated too. She rested her elbows on her knees and her head on her hands and let out a sigh. An idea flashed, she sat up whip-fast and straight. She grabbed Asher by the shoulders and said, almost yelled really, "Hey, what about the Streetcar?"

The pressure of the day steamed off a bit with Lucie's improvement to the plan. "Yeah, that's a great idea." He looked down at the map again. "Oh look Lucie, we could use the Streetcar from here to here," he said pointing to the two locations with the greatest distance between them. The Portland Streetcar was a jump-on, jump-off style railcar that ran on tracks throughout downtown Portland. It would save them time and energy and it was free.

They went on like this for another few minutes, coming up with a timeline and method of seeing fourteen locations in one afternoon, all after lunch but before dinner. Lucie even thought about roller skating, but they quickly rejected that idea when they imagined what it would be like trying to jump on the moving Streetcar with roller skates. They had their plan, and it was time now to go about the regular part of their day, taking care of chores and being the kids their parents expected them to be. This would give Asher his opportunity to go to the garden once again and he slipped into thoughts of the new-found, wondrous place as he stayed quietly by his closest of friends. Asher sat for a moment lost in the thought of his extraordinary colliding spheres of being—one foot on Earth, as it were, and one foot in some kind of law-of-physics-breaking garden of ensorcelling insects and plants and bad guys. Lucie saw this look in Asher's eyes and asked, "What, what is it?"

In the briefest and tiniest of tiny, brief moments, Asher almost told her everything; in fact he had *decided* to tell her everything. This was Lucie—he never kept anything from Lucie. He was going to tell her about the bugs, and the garden and how they were like people and how he could "travel" through time and space or something like that and before a single word came out, he changed his mind. "I was just wondering what we would do with Simon if we couldn't live here."

Lucie could tell that he was keeping something from her by the way he said it, with his eyes averted and his halted speech. "It's okay Asher, you know your dad will find a way to make sure you are near Simon and that he'll be well taken care of." She was discomfited as she said this, only because she didn't understand why Asher would have lied to her. Did he know something he wasn't telling her? She decided that she trusted him and that whatever it was, not telling her must be the right thing; how could it not be? This was Asher; she trusted him. "I'm going to go do my chores now so I can be back, and we can get going." She stood up and waited for him to look at her. He finally lifted his head.

"See you later."

"See ya," and she turned without a smile on her face. Lucie was the type of person who always smiled unless she was angry or hurt, and she was almost never hurt, but she did not look angry this time. He felt bad for not knowing how to handle this the right way.

Asher made his way to the floor of his deck, leaning against the planter box of San Marzano Romas and closed his eyes, thinking of just himself and the plants, just like Mrs. N. had taught him... think... think. *Nothing except me and the plants. I'm going to see plants, and bugs and no more deck, no more apartment, no car sounds in the street. Just dirt, just big bugs and a big garden and...* and he was spinning madly in the nothingness, pulled and twisted and flying so quickly but not moving at all. Just as he was twisted and spun to his limit in the darkness, he was standing still and perfectly fine in the middle of the big bugs' garden. It was easier this time for him; it registered in his too-smart, twelve-year-old brain that he was getting better at moving between the two places and then wondered what else was possible if this was possible.

Asher saw Halfwing and Spots seated at a table next to a small building that sat adjacent to the garden with tomatoes. They were talking in close proximity to one another and unaware that Asher was now just a few yards away, or so he thought. Halfwing turned and motioned him over, almost irritated with the need to do so, as if she had already expected him to be by their side. She did know he was there, even without looking. He went to them hurriedly, his heart fluttering wildly and his breathing fast; he recognized that he was still excited by this new, and maybe magical, place. He was seated now next to the two bugs.

"Hi, what's going on?" He really didn't know what else to say.

He mostly felt comfortable, but also a bit out of place.

Spots explained, "Legs and Eyes are takin' Digger an' the Boss to check things out at the Paint'n Man's place. We know he's got Leaf in there, and we think that maybe Digger can get him out by diggin' in, findin' him and bringin' him out."

"Do you think I might be able to help somehow?" Asher asked.

"I have a feeling you might," said Halfwing, "but we're not sure how yet. We think that maybe the Painting Man might be afraid of you; I believe he can sense your power. But even if he were afraid of you, we're not sure what to do with that. He has hundreds of slaves who do whatever he wants; they are afraid of what he might do to them."

"How do you know all this?" Asher asked.

"Legs and Eyes," said Spots, "they're the best at gettin' in and out without bein' seen. They're amazin'."

"What do they do?" asked Asher.

"Ya ever heard of a Ghillie suit?" Spots asked Asher.

"Yeah, snipers and hunters have been using Ghillie suits for a couple of centuries now, started in Britain, but it could have also been Africa, no one's really sure. But how do you know about those?"

"I don't know. I just do, kinda like how we always just been here. Anyways, those two can make Ghillie suits faster than you could pick your nose and eat it too!"

"Spots!!" scolded Halfwing.

"Oh, sorry. I mean, they can make Ghillie suits real fast."

"With their webs? And then they do some sort of reconnaissance?" Asher began to figure it out now. Eyes and Legs could probably do many things, all of which, he was sure, would be astonishing by human standards.

They all turned as they heard movement from the trees, and suddenly two huge black masses came flying from midway up the nearest set of trees down toward the three of them. Asher screamed and jumped behind Spots.

"Whoa there kid, it's alright, it's just Legs an' the rest of 'em." he said with a loud guffaw.

Asher looked over Spots' shoulder and saw that the two spiders had rigged seat and harness systems out of webbing and had them slung and strapped across their backs. They scrambled on each of their eight legs lightning-fast across the remaining space with their cargo safely atop them. With a sudden stop only a few feet away, they bent forward making it easy for the passengers to climb off. He recognized Digger and… "Oh my gosh…" Asher was stunned into silence and paralysis.

Spots said, "Asher, you know these three already, and this here is the Boss."

"Nice to meet you," said the Boss as he held his hand toward Asher, who still didn't move and seemed unable to speak. "Hey, Asher, you okay?"

Asher looked into the Boss' eyes. *He doesn't know me? I can't breathe; what do I do? What can I say? Why doesn't he know me?*

Asher was lost. He barely pulled himself together enough to say, "Umm…hi, I'm Asher," and leaned forward to shake the Boss' hand. Then he doubled over and threw up, startling everyone. He fell instantly into the swirling nothingness and was in his own garden again, sitting against the tomato planter box. He sat there and burst into tears, uncontrollable, messy, and sobbing. He lost his strength to even just sit there so he allowed himself to fall to his side and lay his head on his arm. All he could think about as the tears and snot dripped to his arm and matted his hair was to wonder how his own brother, Simon, had gotten into the garden-world and become their boss and...*why didn't Simon recognize me?*

The Child in Him is Missing

Asher had to go back and see Simon again. Right away. He pushed himself back up from the floor of the deck, wiped his face on the front of his shirt and pushed back his hair out of his eyes. He had stopped crying. He wasn't really sure why he was crying; he wasn't really sad. He was just... *what is it? Overwhelmed? Confused? Startled?* He knew, for certain, that he needed to find a way to get Simon to remember who he was, that they were brothers and that he belonged in the real world, or this world; maybe the garden-world is as real as this one he thought. No matter what the case was, he had to go back now, so he closed his eyes and began to think... spinning, twirling, bright darkness... he was there.

Definitely getting easier.

He was there in front of the bugs and his brother again, or the Boss as Simon seemed to only be known there. They were all perplexed by his disappearing act. "I'm sorry that I left again, everyone. I can't seem to really control staying here all that well I guess." He tasted what he thought was spoiled milk in his mouth, then he remembered what happened before he left earlier. He looked down and immediately stepped back from the old and stinking contents of his stomach. "Sorry about that too! I don't know what happened."

"What did happen, my friend?" Digger asked. Spots hit him on the back of his head and said, "He just told you, he doesn't know!"

Halfwing hit Spots and said, "Be kind!"

"That was a great way to say, 'Nice to meet you,'" said Simon and then the rest of them chortled.

"Umm... I guess I'm just not used to going back and forth like that, it must make my stomach queasy; then, when I didn't know it was you guys coming from the trees, it scared me and that just made it worse." By the way that Halfwing was looking at him, he thought that maybe she could sense his half-truth, but the others all accepted it. Soon, they were seated in a circle with the four scouts telling them what they saw.

Eyes started, "Legs, the Boss, and I were hiding in the nearest trees, obscured by branches. It was quite far, but we could make out just where Digger popped up."

Legs added, "I got closer last night, and found the best place for Digger to go under and then come back up. Those guards must feel pretty secure in there because they leave a lot of areas unwatched. Nothing must have ever really threatened them before."

Now Digger shared what he found, "I'm not sure, but I think I know where they are keeping Leaf. There are a set of structures behind the largest central building that look like prison cells. It was dark in each of them and I could just barely see that they were filled with grubs. The guards that watched over the cells were also grubs, but a couple near the middle had other kinds of bugs. A beetle in one and I couldn't see the other, but I thought the shape was similar to an ant, so I think it's Leaf.

"I would have dug into there, right then, but the guards would have heard me. I'm not so sure how we are going to get him out. I can get into the Painting Man's compound, but I can't move around all that well without running the risk of getting caught."

"We'll have to attack this problem from different angles I think," said Simon, the Boss. "We could come up with some way to distract them or lure them away from the cells. We could have Digger get Leaf out of there then over the walls on Legs' or Eyes' back. Do you think you could draw us a map of the compound Digger?"

"No, not well enough, I'll need to see more."

"Maybe between what you know and what the spiders know, we can put one together, it would be best if we didn't go back so often," said the Boss.

Asher now saw why Simon had become the Boss. Asher may have come more naturally to academic study, but Simon always won when they played chess, or checkers, or Battleship, or Risk, despite the fact that he was two years younger. Simon understood football and basketball and watched them intently with their father; to Asher, it just looked like a big mess of people chasing after a ball, no different from schoolyard keep-away. This was natural to Simon, like some children are naturals at music or gymnastics; Simon was a strategist and could "see" the big picture of how things would work. Asher thought that Simon would probably learn military strategy easier than the ABC's. So here he was now, seemingly with nothing left of himself but that one aspect—he was now only a strategist; he might be ten years old, but he was definitely the Boss. The only thing that Asher could think of that was similar to what's happening to his brother was *Lord of the Flies*, and now he was worried that Simon could lose his humanity if he never remembered who he was.

"Hey Boss," Asher said, "I think that I understand what you're saying but there's a problem. If the guards are wood-eating grubs, they'll have huge mandibles that would crush any one of us if we get too close while we try to distract them." Asher was happy to have input, but more so, he just wanted to talk to his brother.

"We'll be faster and keep our distance; all we have to do is make it look like there's a problem that all the guards need to go take care of."

"What are you thinking?" Asher asked.

"Yeah, there aren't that many of us here," said Legs, "It's not like we're an army an' there are hundreds of them. I understand what you're saying, but I don't see how we can do it." Legs was mostly a pessimist, but it kept everyone safe since it was usually him who saw flaws in plans and ideas.

"Why can't we be an army? I'm sure we can figure something out. We have other ants in that part of the garden." Simon, the Boss, pointed behind the nearby tomato bed to a far set of crops, and some other small buildings, barely huts really, "I'm sure if we keep it simple we could get a couple dozen of them to help us out, and we could maybe rig something up that you and Eyes could build."

Asher could see the wheels turning in Simon's mind. Simon had the basic idea of a plan but now Asher knew where he could help. "I can come up with a design, I think. If we make one person look like three or four, we can take ten people and make them look like forty. And if we do it exactly right, we could take that forty and make them look like the front of a large regiment."

"I like your kind o' thinkin'." Spots said to Asher, "But how are we gonna do that?"

They all looked at Asher now. "We'll have to talk about it later, I have to go now, but if you get a big map drawn, I can show you some things when I get back. I'll design it so that Legs and Eyes can build it. Then the Boss can come up with a plan of attack using them."

"Can we do anything now?" asked Legs and Eyes together at the same time, and it reminded Asher that they were father and daughter.

"If you guys could have fifty or sixty sticks of various lengths made between now and tonight, I'll be able to come up with something that will use them." Asher didn't know what yet, but he understood that with good webbing and straight sticks, he could probably build the garden-world version of the Eiffel tower; it wouldn't be too different from playing with the Erector sets his mom and dad got for him every Christmas. "I gotta go now, but I'll be back tonight." He waved and they all waved back. He looked at Simon and almost lost it again, but he closed his eyes and thought about home; he realized that he had never voluntarily left the garden-world before and wondered if he actually could. The sudden spinning and twirling into nothing told him that he could. This time again, it did not take as long, nor was it as disorienting. He opened his eyes to his own garden on his deck, looked at the time and knew he had to meet his father for lunch. First, he had to go and talk to Mrs. Neighbors.

*****

He jumped up and tore through his apartment and across the hall. Halted at the doorway and very excitedly said "Hi Mrs. Neighbors! May I come in please? I need to talk to you right now."

"Come in son. I'm here in the..." but she stopped because Asher was already in front of her. "... the living room, but it looks like you had no trouble finding me. Not like I'd be all that good at hiding in this little apartment of mine, what with all the clutter and my old body's inability to, well, move at all, really."

"Mrs. N., you won't believe this. I found Simon in the garden-world."

"Is that what we're going to call it? The garden-world? I think I like that, son."

"Mrs. N.! Did you hear me?! Simon's in the garden-world!!"

"I know. I know son. Why do you think I've been telling you it's so important that we keep this place and that you go back there and help them with their problems in the garden-world? Simon has been stuck there for a year now."

"How did you know?" Asher was hurt and shocked that Mrs. Neighbors had kept this from him for so long. Alta Neighbors sensed his feelings.

"Asher, son, listen to this old lady and you give her the respect she deserves."

"Yes, ma'am."

"How would you have reacted if I came to you a year ago and said that Simon's mind and spirit are trapped in a world that you can't see, but you can get to it through your garden, but only if you can find a way to connect to it in your mind powerfully enough to carry you there, and that's why he's stuck in his coma that seems to be affected by unusual brain activity?"

"I guess I would have told my dad that maybe we need to send you to a nursing home for the mentally unstable." He wasn't being flippant; that really was what he thought he would do in that scenario.

"So, I knew Simon was there because I could feel him there. Just like I explained to you before."

"But Mrs. N. He doesn't know who he is; he doesn't recognize me either. What do I do?"

133

Her lips pursed as she contemplated this hitch. "I don't know son. But that explains some things. I could always sense him there, but there was something different about it, kind of like the child part of him was gone, but he was still there. This could be trouble. I believe you can go there and back, because you are aware of both places, and the fact that the garden-world came out of your own pain and shock on that vicious day makes it easier I'm sure."

"I get that. So if he can't remember who he is, then he won't be able to come back. He has to want to be back, but he can only want what he knows."

"Yes son, you do understand the problem, quite clearly. Your mother did not raise fools."

"I think that I'm going to go see Simon at the care center today. After lunch with Dad."

"I think that would be a good idea."

*****

Somewhere near the blackened heart of the Painting Man's keep, a short and stout grub-soldier was explaining to his lord that he did not find the worm as he was ordered to do.

Moments later, there was nothing left of him but a pile of smoking, greasy ash.

Derek Rey

Statues and Silver Eyes

Asher was almost late meeting his father at J.J's for lunch, running downstairs after taking a couple of minutes to wash his face a little better and brush his hair back. He then changed his shirt after noticing how dirty it was from wiping his nose on the front of it earlier that morning.

Lunch went quickly, with Asher hurrying his father by pretending that he wanted to go and play with Lucie; though really, he knew that he and Lucie had even less time this afternoon to visit all the properties that they had planned on visiting since he was going to go and see Simon. That charade was unmasked when Asher started to follow his father to go see Simon instead of turning into Harper's Market to go knock on Lucie's front door.

"Asher, are you coming with me to see Simon? I thought you were going to go play with Lucie." Ray Jakes was pleasantly surprised. He had worried about his son's aversion to seeing his little brother but had chosen not to think about it on the urgings of a wise Mrs. Neighbors late one evening, soon after the accident. Ray took Asher's momentary behavior change as a gift.

"Umm… I don't know Dad, I guess 'cause it's summertime so I've been thinking about him," which was partially true.

"Okay, I probably shouldn't look a gift horse in the mouth."

Ray and Asher went into Simon's room together and Asher helped Ray adjust Simon in his bed, looking for bed sores and redness, and fussing over this and that. Asher sat quietly across from his father, who was sitting on a stool, leaning toward his still son. Asher watched how his father had preened and now looked at Simon. He could see that his father was thinking things that hurt deeply but somehow also sated something in his reeling heart. Twice he saw that his dad must have been remembering a specific time and memory based on his body language and facial expressions while staying mute, almost as if he was having a thought-conversation with Simon.

He didn't want to interrupt this moment his brother and father had together, but he also felt a need to get going. He needed to talk to Simon, and he needed to go meet Lucie and what he wanted to say to Simon he couldn't say with his father present.

"Dad, do you think you could give me a minute with Simon?"

Ray was slightly taken aback, but he was not upset, "Sure. I can do that for you." He got up and walked around the bed toward the door, then turned back and gave his son a squeeze on the shoulder with one of his big hands, a squeeze that said so much more than 'I love you' and Asher felt it as much as his father meant it. Then Ray left.

Asher stood by Simon now, close enough to hold his near hand and lay his other on his brother's shaved head. "Simon!" he said urgently but quietly. "Simon! I found you. I'm going to help you get back, I promise. I will get you back here." Asher didn't know if Simon could hear him at all, and he didn't think so since most of Simon was in the garden-world, unaware of this other reality. He looked for some type of response anyway. "I hope you can hear me, at least a little." Still nothing. "I want you to hear my voice. It's me Asher, you are Simon. You are my brother. We live in Portland with our dad." It was now that Asher understood something terrible. Simon didn't know that their mother had died.

It stabbed Asher in the gut to think about telling this to Simon, but he had to. "Simon, I have to tell you something. Mom… umm…" He thought about not telling him, but it was easier this way, when Simon had no response. "Umm… Mom… Mom died, Simon." Asher was holding himself back now. He didn't want to cry again. He felt he had to be the strong one for his brother, who was surely going to need everything that his big brother could give to him, like their father did for him a year ago.

"Simon, Mom died in a car accident." He choked on these words. "You were in it too." He was losing it now. "You got really hurt and now you're in a place that I don't think you belong in." Only half his words were audible, the rest a garbled, mash of half-words and sobs. "I can help you get back, but only if you remember who you are, and who I am, and where your home and your family are."

Asher looked for any sign of a response, did the monitors flicker, did his temperature rise, or his heartbeat quicken? Did his hand move? No. Nothing.

"Simon, I'm coming to get you, I promise. I will get you home. I promise more than anything I've ever promised before, I'll get you home."

Asher held his brother's hand for a moment longer. He laid his head on his brother's chest and listened to his heartbeat. He just wanted to hear life in his brother in any form that he could observe.

"I promise."

Then he went to get Lucie.

He went to his bedroom to get the map of Portland with the markings they had made earlier that morning. He grabbed the funnel-phone, "Lucie, you there?"

Whoosh, he heard the pulling of the hose on the other end. "Yeah, I've been waiting for you for-EVER! What took you so long?! We might not get to all the places now."

"We don't have a choice, we have to. I'm sorry, I just…" he wasn't prepared to lie to Lucie again, "I just had to go with my Dad to see Simon."

He hoped she wouldn't ask why.

She paused then said, "Okay, let's just get going, I'll meet you at the corner of the market." Lucie knew something was going on that he wasn't telling her. This was the first time he had gone to see Simon in weeks. She thought he would have told her he was going to visit him.

He was thankful that she didn't ask, but he could tell that she thought something was going on. "See ya in a minute".

Clink.

Clink.

And he was out the door. He met Lucie on the corner like she asked and they quickly started walking toward 13th Avenue where two buildings on their list sat near each other, five blocks west and one block south would take them to the first place, just off the northwest corner of Portland State University.

They made it there in just a few minutes, half walking, half running. They got to the building and saw that it was an old church that had been abandoned years before. They both recognized it and knew the building well. It was one of those buildings that stuck out among what was around it for several reasons; it was the only empty building on the block, it was dark stone from old masonry while the adjacent buildings featured modern architectural pops, and large glass windows and walls. It had large red, arched front doors. It was also the only building with ivy growing at least partially on all four sides.

It was kind of a scary building, one you wouldn't want to go into, even on a dare, Asher thought. But these two were not doing a dare; they were on a mission. They stepped up to the building's front doors and tried to peek through the crack in the middle. No luck. There must have been some kind of overlap on the inside that they couldn't see past. They walked around the side of the building. There wasn't much room between it and the next building over, but the next building had no windows on this side, so they felt somewhat safe; at least no one would probably see them poking around. Lucie saw a window that she thought she could see in if she sat on Asher's shoulders, so that was what they did. She reported what she saw.

"There's a little bit of light. I can see almost everything. The light is coming from windows up high on the walls. It's dusty in there, I don't think that Breitel has even been in here."

"What other things do you see?"

"It's just one big room. The walls are painted with things from the Bible. All the pews are pushed to one corner of the room. The place where the priest, or maybe the pastor stood is clear too. But there's a statue in the middle of the room."

"A statue? Like the Virgin Mary or something?"

"Nope, you should look at this, it's just a statue of a guy. He looks like he might be wearing jeans and carrying a backpack."

"What?" Now Asher's curiosity was piqued. He practically dropped Lucie trying to get her off of his shoulders. Luckily, she landed on her feet and stabilized herself by grabbing some nearby ivy that was climbing up the wall. She put her hands on her knees and did a squatted stance so that Asher could step on her leg then over her shoulder. It had been a while since she had tried to hold

Asher on her shoulders and it had not gone well, but she was older and stronger and had lifted many more crates of fruits and vegetables since then, so she was confident. Asher on the other hand was doubtful.

"Hurry up Asher, we have thirteen more places to go and I think you should see that statue!" Up he went and she had no problem with it.

What he saw made no sense to him. The statue was stone, but clearly smoothed over and it had a good sheen to the finish. It was new, or at least, it was recently polished. But a regular looking guy with a backpack? Why would there be such a statue. He didn't look rich, or powerful, or saintly—he was simply a regular guy. 'Regular' was the best word. There was something about that stance, the clothes that kind of looked familiar but Asher had never seen this statue before.

He saw what he needed to see and asked Lucie to let him down. They left the small space between the buildings and headed north on 13th Avenue. Four blocks away was the second building, again abandoned and empty.

This building looked like it had probably been a business of some sort that maybe had apartments upstairs. Big and boxy and nearly half the city block. Faded and sun-bleached yellow paint was mostly present, but not bright as it must have once been. This building was not usable; it was beyond repair. Holes were visible up high, as if heavy winds had torn the siding away and it was never repaired. There was a noticeable sway to the roof; the center must be a full foot lower than the corners. And it was barely perceptible, but the whole building leaned slightly to one side, they didn't see it at first but now that they were looking for more problems, it became obvious. "No trespassing," and "Danger," signs were posted all over.

They found a window and looked into it. The floor to the second floor was missing, but some of the framework was still visible. It was completely open, again—just one big room. Trash was strewn everywhere except for a spot near the center of the building, where it was clear for a diameter of about fifteen feet. In the center of the cleared area was another statue, a lady in a business suit and a briefcase. They could both see it and it confused them more than the first statue. Now they had seen two statues of 'regular' people. Both buildings were obviously in a state of disrepair.

They had no idea what the story was with Breitel and these investment properties, but they didn't want their home to be another one. They continued their journey. The remaining twelve properties looped around the majority of downtown Portland. They crossed over I-405 to 16th Avenue and headed north. By the time they crossed West Burnside Street, a major thoroughfare a half mile north, they had visited two more sites, both in similar condition to the first two, both with statues of regular people. Another man and another woman.

They wended their way to Couch Park using the Streetcar, and then on foot they went east toward the North Park Blocks, which were just like the South Park Blocks, but as the name would suggest, in the north part of downtown Portland. Again, they had seen two more places and they were just the same, but this time, both statues were men. They went east toward the Burnside Bridge and this was the part of the loop that had the most places close together, four buildings to visit over a six-block walk.

They could only see into three buildings and all three buildings had a statue inside. They assumed that the fourth probably did as well. There were two more statues of ladies and one of a man.

They took the bus across the Burnside bridge and walked a fourteen-block path that went near the Oregon Ballet theatre, and close to the Hawthorne Bridge before going back up toward the Morrison Bridge. They had seen three more places on this path and again, two more statues of ladies and another of a man.

They were now standing at a bus stop, waiting for a bus to take them over the bridge toward their last property, which was a couple of blocks south of Morrison St. back toward their home on the South Park Blocks. As they were waiting, Lucie had been looking at the files of the properties. "Hey Asher, I noticed something kind of weird here. The places we visited, they go in order."

"What kind of order, do you mean?"

"Time order, what's the word?"

"Chronological you mean?"

"Yeah, chronological order. You know how it was kind of convenient that all the properties made a loop. Well, it looks like Breitel bought them in that order too. Like he's buying a loop of properties."

"Yeah, but why? He's not really investing, that's obvious. I want to know what he's really doing and what the statues are for."

"Well, it looks like he just bought this last place a couple of weeks ago; maybe something will be different here."

Then the bus came, and not wanting to draw any attention, they didn't talk on the bus. After they got off on the other side of the bridge, they hopped on the Streetcar again and headed south, going three blocks in about a minute and a half until they arrived at their final property. There were no free-standing buildings here that were like the other thirteen properties. There was however a portion of a building on a slightly less busy street that had paper up against the windows and doors so no one could see into it. It looked like it should be empty, or at least, not in use for the immediate future. They weren't sure if this was really the place. The address was not clear and the description sort of fit, but there was a lot of language describing it that the two children simply could not understand.

They tried to peek through small rips in the paper and at the edges of the paper where it didn't overlap cleanly. No real luck. But then a few feet to their side, the door opened, startling them. Out walked a tall man, very powerful-looking in a business suit that had to have been tailored considering how perfectly it seemed to fit him. His hair was perfect too, dark and groomed and they thought it looked like a businessman or politician would have it.

"Hello. How are you?" the man said as he was buttoning his cuffs.

They stumbled over their words, startled by unexpectedly running into someone, let alone having that someone talk to them. "Umm…uh… okay, we're fine sir, thank you."

As the door swung closed behind the man, Asher saw that there was a statue in there. Another regular looking man, this one in a business suit, but not a nice one like the one on the tall man who stood before him now.

"Are you with your parents?" the tall man asked. His eyes were silver, and they penetrated the two children like ancient daggers.

Lucie shook her head. Asher said with his voice shaking, "We were looking for a place to get some food, we got our allowances today and wanted to try something new."

"Your parents aren't with you then?"

This time, both children just shook their heads.

The tall man came over and crouched so he could look them straight-on. They could feel his breath, he leaned so close. "Children, this is not a restaurant, or a candy store. It is not open for business of any kind. And who knows, I may not be a nice man. You'd better run off before something happens to you; this is a dangerous world and time we live in." He reached up and pinched their cheeks like an aunt might, but it felt like a threat, not a sign of affection, and his smile was surely not of the kind sort. "Go home, go now." He stood up and turned and locked the door to the space from which he came, the one with the fourteenth statue in it.

The two children were already running toward home when the tall man turned back around, gazing in their direction.

Lucie Through the Funnel

They were up in Asher's apartment now. They went into his bedroom where they felt safest.

"Asher, I know who that was. I saw him get out of a Limousine and talk to my dad a few days ago, but I didn't really think much about it because he bought some stuff from the market. I just figured he was being polite when he was talking to my dad about the market before buying his food because sometimes people like to do that with my dad 'cause he's good at talking to customers you know, I mean he gets a lot of practice doing it every day so of course he's…"

"Lucie, who is it?!"

"It's Breitel! It has to be. He was at my dad's market and now he's at that place."

"I thought it might be, I haven't seen him before though. But there's something different about him too. You remember when he got really close to us. It seemed like he was trying to say something to us without saying it. Adults don't normally talk to kids like that."

"No, I thought he was trying to read my mind the way he was looking at me with those scary eyes," Lucie said.

"Lucie, there has to be something with those statues. What do you think it might be? I can't figure anything out. But I did see one in that last building too. Right when Breitel had stepped out, I saw it for just a second."

"I don't know what's going on with those; I've been thinking about it all day too and I can't figure it out either."

They heard footsteps coming up the stairs and figured it was Asher's father when they looked at the clock. He'd be coming home to pick Asher up for dinner. They got up and met him in the living room. "Dad, you ready for dinner?" Asher asked.

"You bet I am kiddo. Long afternoon on the phone, typing and re-typing. It just wasn't coming together all that well today. I just want to relax and eat now."

"Can I come Mr. Jakes?" Lucie said with cloying sweetness, though she didn't have to because Ray would never turn her down.

"Just ask your parents first."

Lucie ran out of their apartment and bounded down the stairs. Asher and Ray headed out as well and stopped by Mrs. Neighbors' apartment and looked in on her. Ray said, "Mrs. N., we're going to J.J.'s; you want anything or you want to come with us, maybe?"

"What does he have for dinner tonight?"

"Normal stuff, plus pot roast on mashed potatoes."

"Pot roast repeats on me, son. What does he have for soup?"

"Beer cheese."

"That's what I'll have. Ask him for some garlic bread to go with it, would you?"

"Will do. We'll be back in a little bit."

By the time Asher and Ray had walked in the door to J.J.'s, Lucie was by their side. Within a few moments they were in and seated and three orders of pot roast were on the table. All three of them were preoccupied tonight as they ate their food. It was Lucie though who began to tap Asher's leg under the table and motion her head toward the television.

"Well Jenny, only two days later and there is another

'disconnect' found. A man was discovered sitting on this curb at the corner of 1ˢᵗ and Yamhill. He was immediately identified as Dwayne Singler, a lawyer who does pro bono work as a public defender. Being within mere blocks of the Multnomah county courthouse, a passerby on his way to a lunch recognized him and stopped to say 'Hi', but then realized that he was the newest victim of this strange phenomenon."

"Tell me Matthew, is there still no word from OHSU about what might be causing this?"

"No Jenny, none whatsoever. The CDC did say that they have ruled out anything chemical, which is a blessing and a curse, apparently. Since it's not chemical-related, all city resources will remain undisturbed. If it were chemical-related, there would have been an immediate and indefinite shut-off of the water supply."

"Well that's good news then Matthew."

"Yes Jenny, it is, but it's also bad news. Since it's not a chemical causing this, the CDC and OHSU are at a loss for which direction to take in the investigation now. They believe that it could be some kind of shared traumatic experience, but they don't know what it could possibly be, since most likely, whatever would have caused this would have been noticeable and discovered by this time."

"Thank you, Matthew, we'll talk to you again later."

"Thank you, Jenny, for KCMW, this has been Matthew Maxwell."

Normally, Lucie did not pay attention to the news, in print or on television, but this caught her attention because in the background was the building in which she and Asher saw the fourteenth statue. As the newscast went to commercial, Asher and Lucie looked at each other with renewed fear. It felt like such a strange coincidence that the location of the disturbing encounter they had less than an hour earlier was now on the news, on television.

"Are you two alright?" Ray asked. "You hardly ever pay attention to the news. Last time I saw you watching the news, Asher, was when Stephen Hawking came to town."

"We were just wondering about those disconnected people on the news, Dad. We were talking about them today is all and now there's a story on the news about it tonight. That's all." Asher was apparently getting more comfortable lying to his father, but that didn't make him feel any better about it.

"Asher, Lucie, you shouldn't worry yourselves about that kind of thing. It's my job to worry about that for you while you go out and have fun, okay?" Ray said this with care and maybe a little fear. He wasn't belittling the children; he was just being protective. "Looks like you two are just about done. Let's get going."

They left the restaurant with their plates cleaned off; Lucie had even licked her plate clean at the very end while professing the greatness of J.J.'s gravy. Ray grabbed the to-go bag for Mrs. Neighbors and Asher grabbed a small left over piece of pot roast in case the grey-and-black tabby was outside again tonight, which it was. It rubbed up against Asher's leg right as he stepped outside the door, a brand-new old friend, apparently. Asher dropped the piece of pot roast near the wall to keep the tabby out of the way of passersby and it ate slowly and peacefully. Asher thought that it was watching him walk away.

Soon, they were inside and up the stairs. "Dad, Lucie and I are going to go play around back in my room. Okay?"

"That's fine, leave the door open so you can hear me if I call, I'm going to sit with Mrs. N. for a while."

"Okay dad."

"Thanks, Mr. Jakes," Lucie added.

The two ran to his room, jumped on the bed and both started in about the news story, words tumbling and careening into each other so that neither heard what the other was saying. Finally, Asher said, "Wait, wait..." and held a hand up. Lucie stopped. "Okay, here's what I think, Lucie. Breitel is doing something that might be illegal since he's obviously not doing anything with the properties that he said he was going to do. That tells me that he's hiding something. We have to figure out what it is."

"How are we going to do that? We hardly understand the papers we do have, and I have no idea where to begin to figure out what he's really up to."

"We need Jenny's help again."

"Yeah, but we weren't supposed to go and look at those properties, remember?"

"That's not a problem; we'll tell Mrs. N. about what we found, and she can tell Jenny about it. Then Jenny will know how to do more digging for us."

"Okay, then, I guess there's nothing else for us to do tonight until we talk to Mrs. N. Your dad will be with her for a while, so we won't get to talk with her until tomorrow morning," Lucie said disappointedly. She was not ready to be done with this tonight; she felt like they were just getting going. "Umm... what now?"

"I don't know, Lucie." But Asher did know, he wanted to go back to the garden and he also wanted to tell Lucie all about the garden.

Lucie noticed the far-off look in Asher's eyes—he was somewhere in his mind right now, and Lucie wanted to know where. "What are you thinking about Asher? You look like when Mrs. Good asks a question, and you don't know the answer."

Asher almost told her again, "Umm… I… need to take care of the garden."

"I'll help you. You look like you wanted to say something else anyway and we can talk about it while we work on the garden."

"NO!" he yelled. "I mean… no," he said more softly. "It's okay, I'll take care of it." He was tearing inside with every half-truth he told her. "There's nothing else I wanted to say; I was just thinking about… the garden. That's all."

"Fine! You can take care of it yourself then!" She got up and left without looking back.

Asher didn't know how to respond. He heard her stomping down the stairs. He heard her front door slam through his window. He leaned over and put his ear to the funnel-phone. He could just barely hear her enter her room, but it was unmistakable that she was now crying.

*****

Lucie didn't know why Asher was keeping something from her. She wasn't sure why she couldn't keep it together. She hated crying. She had been mad at him before and didn't cry like this. Maybe it was because she was losing her home. Maybe because she was losing her friend. All she knew was that she was upset at everything and the last thing she needed was for her best friend to be hiding something from her.

A Cat Named Dude

It was a tradition in the Harper household that Lucie would sit by her mother on the couch before bed and ask her father about how business that day went. She liked hearing about all the people he met. She like hearing that people bought her favorite fruits and vegetables. She felt badly for the fruits and vegetables that didn't sell well. Without siblings, this was her natural way of connecting with her only family.

As she came in the door, she slammed it behind her. She threw her shoes in the closet by the front door and stomped back to her bedroom and slammed that door as well. Mrs. Harper wasn't sure, but she thought she saw Lucie wipe tears from her cheek, although she definitely heard her sniffle. Mr. and Mrs. Harper looked at one another, concern reflecting back to each. Mrs. Harper shrugged and said, "I'll go see." Mr. Harper nodded without a word and watched his wife head back to their daughter's room. Even though his favorite show, "Hill Street Blues," was on, he couldn't take his eyes away from the hallway that led to where Mrs. Harper went. He bit his calloused thumb and sat there, just staring.

knock knock knock

Lucie heard her mother rapping on her bedroom door. She didn't respond. Her mother turned the handle and stepped in. Lucie buried her face in her pillow. She heard her mother take a few steps and then felt her sit on her bed beside her.

Mrs. Harper reached down and started twirling Lucie's hair in her fingers. "Do you want to talk about it, honey?"

"No."

"Okay."

"Asher is making me mad!" After a short moment, Lucie reached to her bedside, grabbed a couple of tissues, and stuffed them in her end of the funnel-phone. She turned and her mother could see her red, wet cheeks and bloodshot eyes. "Something's bothering him and he won't tell me what it is and I'm his best friend and what are best friends for anyway if we're not gonna be the people you can talk to when there's stuff bothering you because that's exactly what best friends are for except he won't tell me what's bothering him and he even tries to pretend that NOTHING is bothering him when it's so obvious that something IS bothering him so what is it? Is it me? Did I do something? How would I know? He won't tell me! So now he's taking care of his garden by himself and he told me I couldn't help him and this is the FIRST TIME EVER he said I couldn't help him with the garden and I'm just really upset!"

Mrs. Harper took a breath and let it out with a subtle sigh. "Honey, do you still consider Asher to be your best friend?"

"Yes."

"Do you think he still considers you his best friend?"

"NO!"

"Are you sure?"

"Okay, yes."

"What has he been dealing with the last couple of days?"

"A lot."

"And don't forget, it was last summer when the accident

happened, and summer just started. There are probably some painful and confusing feelings he doesn't even realize he has right now."

"Yeah, okay. Maybe."

Mrs. Harper let a silent moment pass. She could see Lucie coming around even if it was just a little. "Remember when you were eight years old and we got you a kitten? You named him Dude."

"Yeah. Dude was so pretty."

"Do you remember how Dude got sick and died and then you didn't want another cat after that?"

"Yeah."

"Do you remember that you got in trouble and got grounded a few days later?"

"Yeah."

"Why?"

Lucie looked away but spoke softly, "I got mad at Dad and then I went out to the market and pushed over the watering cart."

"Why were you mad at him?"

"Because he said my haircut was cute."

"What did you tell your father after you were sent to your room?"

"I told him that I was sorry. That I didn't really mean it. I wasn't actually mad at him and I didn't know why I was mad. I thanked him for saying my haircut was cute. Then I started to tell him that I missed Dude and wanted him back."

"And..."

"He held me while I was crying about Dude. I hate crying."

"Even after that, how did you feel?"

"Still bad. And I didn't want to talk about it because it would make me cry and I hate crying."

"Do you see, honey?"

Lucie looked up at her mother for a moment, waiting for more explanation. She saw a look on her mother's face that said she wasn't going to say any more. Then, "Oh. I get it." She looked down and felt guilty; it came rushing all at once. His mother, his brother, their home, he might lose the garden… "I'll talk to Asher tomorrow morning. I'll let him know he can have my help if he wants it but it's okay if he doesn't." She knew Asher would already be tending the garden tonight anyway.

*****

Asher knew that Lucie wouldn't want him to know she was crying so he pulled away from the funnel-phone. He thought once more about calling her and telling her everything. He couldn't bring himself to do it. How could she believe him? He wondered how many times Mrs. Neighbors wanted to tell him about Simon but couldn't bring herself to do it either.

Asher gathered together a sleeping bag, a pillow, and some snacks and told his dad that he was going to sleep on the deck to watch the meteor shower.

"What meteor shower?"

"Geez Dad, the tau Herculeids are peaking tonight and tomorrow."

"You probably won't be able to see them. Too much light from the city."

"But there could be small fireballs and I would be able to see those."

"Well okay then…would you like me to sleep out there w…"

"NO!!! Uhh…you should probably get some good sleep so that you can write well tomorrow."

Asher didn't think his dad would buy it.

He didn't. "What are you up to, kid?"

"Uhh…I just wanted to be out there alone tonight. After seeing Simon today… I don't know. I just want to be alone and last year he and I watched these together so…"

"Alright. But if you change your mind, let me know."

Asher had everything set up. His sleeping bag was right up against the box of Romas. There weren't any tomatoes yet, but he could see some of the buds and their tiny yellow tips just forming. He focused in on the buds and thought about the other garden. He imagined Spots and Halfwing. He imagined standing in front of his brother.

Swirling and whirling blackness…

"…and this team of ants will come from the north side. They need to stay far enough away from the river so that they aren't seen against the water. Who is going to lead that…oh, Asher. Hi." It was Simon speaking. Asher looked down and saw that there was a map drawn on the surface of a table. They were in a small hut. Spots, Legs, Eyes, Digger, and two ants who he had not yet met, were all around this map. It looked like it was drawn with charcoal.

Asher couldn't believe he was right in front of his brother. The way Simon was talking now reminded Asher of when they would go camping as a family and Simon would try to dictate how and where the campsite needed to be set up. He would draw imaginary

156

maps in the dirt and pretend that he was an army general. He looked more closely at the map on the table and saw that seeds and small stones were placed all over the table-map. It now looked like a game of Risk. Asher would occasionally beat Simon at chess, but Asher could never beat Simon at Risk.

"Hi. Umm, it looks like you're planning something."

"Yeah. The Boss is tellin' us how it's all gonna go down," said Spots. "We're gonna break up into squads or somethin' like that. A couple of 'em will make a big distraction or somethin' then the rest of us are gonna sneak in and get Leaf outta there."

"Let me show you," said Simon the Boss.

Asher stepped forward and looked down at the table. He wanted to say something like, "Sure," or "Okay, what's the plan?" but the words wouldn't come; they were stuck in his throat, afraid of the sight of Simon, afraid they would quiver and belie this false calm Asher put forth. So silent he remained.

Simon continued pointing to a group of seeds on the map, "This is the place on the wall where Legs and I scouted out that we can go over during the distraction. We'll need at least a full minute to get everyone over. Here's where Pharaoh will be leading this group of ants." He pointed to one of the ants as he said this; it had a golden exoskeleton. "Set up about 50 yards from the wall and then light the torches. Asher, they're going to need whatever it is you were thinking about. The distraction thing you were going to show us how to make."

"Oh yeah. I was thinking about this game I use to play with my brother, foosball."

"Okay, what's that?" When Simon said this, it stung Asher and he had to stop himself from wincing.

"It's this game where a bunch of figures of people are on a

rod that is controlled by a player. When the player moves the rod, all of the people move at once."

"Oh, I get it! Legs, Eyes, Pharaoh, this one's all you. Asher, describe the thing to them."

"Well uhh…if we can get something to look like heads with masks and then put them on top of some of those sticks you were going to have ready…"

Legs spoke up, "The ants all got together. We have a couple hundred sticks. Some are short, some long, some a little bent, but mostly, they're straight and strong."

"Good." Asher continued to speak as he picked up a piece of charcoal and started to draw on a small corner of the tabletop. He showed Legs and Eyes that they could use their web and the sticks to build a lattice-type structure. It could be as long as necessary and about the same height as an ant, but if they built enough of them and lined them up, it would look like a regiment of dozens of bugs. In reality, it would only take three or four bugs to carry one row that would then look like fifteen or twenty. Eyes had the idea of using sticky webbing at the top of the lattice, which would allow the ants to then gather leaves and smaller sticks to form what would look like "heads".

Digger then spoke up, "If we attach the torches to this contraption, then we would free up more hands to carry even more rows of this thing."

The Boss spoke up again, "Legs, Eyes, Pharaoh, and Goldy, we can handle the rest on our own here. Get out there and start building. When you're done, meet us back here so that we can set up our part of the plan." The two spiders and two ants all left at once.

After the spiders and ants left, Simon began showing Asher the rest of the plan. When he was done, Asher was fairly certain this would go without a hitch if everything that Simon explained was accurate.

The Quest for Leaf

B ack on the deck above the Park Blocks, Asher's still body lay next to the box of Romas, eyes closed, but not actually asleep.

In the garden-world and under the darkness of night, a few dozen ants along with Legs, Eyes, Digger, Spots, the Boss, and Asher made their way through the bush that lay between the bugs' garden and the compound of the Painting Man. After a short time—short enough that Asher realized that the Painting Man's compound was a little too close for comfort—they left the cover of the bush and entered a clearing. A few hundred yards ahead was the ominous wall with its spiked top and massive torches. Asher could barely make out the Painting Man's soldiers, holding spears and marching along the top of the wall, dark blobs rhythmically moving left and right.

Simon stopped the group. He motioned for Legs and Pharaoh to follow him. They moved a few feet away from the group, hunched down toward the ground, and Simon started to draw in the dirt with a stick, exactly like he used to do when they would go camping as a family. He occasionally pointed toward the Painting Man's compound, and he seemed to mostly be addressing Pharaoh.

A minute or two passed then Pharaoh came back and motioned for Goldy and the rest of the ants to follow. As they marched on in the dark, Asher noticed that they stayed along the line of trees and bushes, going around the left side of the compound toward its northern wall, and he eventually lost sight of them in the dark. As ant after ant marched past, he saw that the lattice structures they carried were larger than he imagined they might be. Thanks to the unbelievable lightness and strength of the webbing from Legs and Eyes, they were able to make lattice soldiers of almost thirty-wide apiece; thanks to the strength of the ants, it only took three ants to carry each of the lattice structures. He did the math and realized that there weren't hundreds of sticks, but instead, there were thousands. He distinctly remembered asking for fifty or sixty sticks.

Eyes saw Asher's expression, "The ants did all the work. My dad and I just provided the webbing. We spooled it on large posts and they went to work building. It took no time. At the end, we just ran along and spotted sticky webbing at the top so they could make the heads."

Asher knew in that moment that there was something special in the abilities that all these bugs possessed. Humans would have taken days to construct what these bugs did in under an hour; their coordination was instinctual and well beyond human capability.

The Boss spoke to the group again. "Legs and Eyes will carry us all to the opposite end of the compound on the south side. It's the least protected place, and once the ants light the torches and start marching their fake army toward the north wall, we should see the grubs all move that direction. That's when we go over."

"I don't think I can get over."

"Don't worry Asher, you'll be on Eyes' back. She'll build you a sling that will hold you there." Asher remembered seeing Simon for the first time on the back of one of the spiders and now he understood.

Simon pointed back to the stick-drawn map of the compound in the dirt. "It's a little way from the wall, but if we're quick, we can get to the cells where Leaf is, break him out, and then get out. Spots, do you remember what comes after that?"

"Yup, I fly over to the ants and let 'em know it's time to go!"

"Remember, quickly and quietly. Once we break open the cell, we won't have any time to spare."

Simon, Asher, and Lucie used to play a game with their other friends from school called Prisoner of War. There were two opposing base camps in a modified game of tag. There were infantry and officers in this game. If you were an officer and were tagged by one of the other team's infantry, you had to go to prison, which was a spot in the other team's base. Team members would try to free the prisoner of war by tagging their teammate back out from the other team's prison. You could only accomplish this if you made a distraction in the form of trying to tag officers of the opposing team. Since Simon was smaller than Asher's and Lucie's other friends, he would often be the sneaky one to go and tag their officers back out as Asher and Lucie would make a scene trying to tag officers from the opposition. Asher could not help but be reminded of their afternoon games of Prisoner of War in the Park Blocks. They would usually play around the rocks. Asher wished they were there now.

Soon, they were moving along silently and blindingly fast, Digger and the Boss on Legs' back, Asher on Eyes' back. Spots was able to half-run, half-fly to keep up with them while staying low enough so he wasn't seen. A minute passed, and Simon tapped Legs' back; they all slowed down and then stopped. They were no more than about seventy-five yards from the wall, just far enough that they were hidden in the darkness—any closer and the grubs would be able to make out their silhouettes in the torch light. Simon stood on Legs' back and looked toward the ants. After a short moment, Simon dropped into the sling on Legs' back. Asher could make out that the ants were beginning to light the torches that they placed on the lattice structures. Line after line of fake soldiers lit up. From this far away, it looked like a massive army and the flames were making that area so bright that everywhere else was black in comparison. It was more massive-looking than the number of grubs that must have been in the Painting Man's compound. Simon stared straight at the wall. Asher followed his little brother's gaze. The grubs were still moving in their rhythmic left-and-right pattern.

Simon began mumbling to himself, "Come on, come on, come on."

Asher asked, "Why are they still staying there?"

"I don't know. They're probably waiting for..." and at this moment the rhythmic left-and-right stopped. They all moved left toward the north wall. Simon waited just a few seconds then said with quiet intensity, "Go!" They were off, even faster than before.

This time Spots flew. When they got to the wall, the spiders crawled right over with Digger, the Boss, and Asher on their backs and Spots simply flew over. Asher realized that other than for blocking a line of sight from outsiders, the wall was pretty pointless if the Painting Man was trying to keep out bugs.

When they got over the wall, Legs and Eyes pressed up against the inside of it. Simon slid off Legs' back, Asher and Digger following suit. Simon began to walk in a low crouch between two buildings nearby. Digger brushed up against Asher and whispered, "Look over there," as he motioned with his head. Asher saw a small hole in the ground. "I came up there and then I was able to find Leaf," a broad smile sweeping across his face. Asher could see he was proud of his contribution to the task.

Following Simon, they rounded a corner of one building and then crept along an alleyway between two rows of small buildings. Asher saw that these were the cells. They made it to the end of the row. No Leaf anywhere to be seen.

"I swear, this is the cell where I found Leaf!" Digger said to the group with shock.

"Damnit! We need to find him," said Simon. "I don't know if we'll have another chance."

Asher remembered that "damnit" was the only curse word that he and his brother were able to utter in their home without getting in trouble.

Simon was angry, but he was focused. This was a more mature version of the Simon Asher remembered. "Eyes, take Asher and Digger. Go back the way we came. Take no more than two minutes and see if you can find out where Leaf is. Spots, go above but keep close to the rooftops and try to stay hidden; see what you can find from up there."

"You got it, Boss."

"Legs and I will go this direction. We'll meet back over the wall where we came from." Simon turned and left.

Legs looked back at his daughter, "You heard the boss, let's not lose any time. Go."

Asher jumped on Eyes' back, Digger slithering along the ground next to them. They went back, turned around the other side of the cells and started down another alleyway between some larger buildings. These ones were windowless and just a single level. Asher guessed that these must be for storage, but then thought that maybe they were the grubs' homes since they preferred darkness and windows would therefore be problematic. Then Asher began to think about the fact that if these were grub-dwellings, maybe there were families of grubs there. Could that be? Wouldn't they become beetles eventually? Did it work that way in this world?

They turned another corner; Eyes suddenly stopped and spread her legs preventing Asher and Digger from moving forward. "It's the Painting Man!" Eyes was shaking.

Asher looked through her legs and saw that there was a tall and muscular man about four or five buildings away. Simon and Legs were in front of him. It looked like they were talking but Legs and Simon were both obviously getting ready to attack, crouched low, Simon's fists clenched. Simon always had a temper. He would even try to take on both Asher and Lucie at the same time. This was the face Asher saw now, the face of anger, absent of reason. Asher was panicking, and Digger had to circle him to keep him steady. All Asher could think was that Simon was going to try to attack this grown man and the Painting Man was so much bigger, so much stronger, he wouldn't even flinch—one swipe and the Painting Man would send the child sprawling and crumbled. "Eyes, do something, do something!"

Eyes ran. She ran fast. She was also silent as she ran but it was too late. Asher could see that the Painting Man heard him and turned toward them. Eyes was blocking his line of sight and obscured most of the Painting Man from his view. As she reached them, Simon lunged at the Painting Man. In that second, a dozen grubs fell from the rooftops of the adjacent buildings. They were all holding clubs and they also had their mandibles held wide. Legs spun a web out that immediately wrapped up Simon. He ran away side-swiping the Painting Man as he went. Eyes turned and sent sticky web flying toward the Painting Man as she also ran away. Legs gathered Asher and Digger and kept going. Asher heard a buzz and saw Spots diving toward the melee of grubs trying to attack Eyes. Legs didn't slow at all, his strength and speed much more than Asher realized. They were over the wall in seconds. Legs kept going, but Asher didn't see Eyes or Spots follow.

Asher yelled, "They're not coming! They're caught."

Legs slowed and then stopped, turning back around. He stood silently watching the top of the wall. Spikes, fire, but no Eyes and no Spots. Five seconds, ten seconds, fifteen… Legs began to walk back slowly. "Get off, stay here." After they were off of Legs, he sped up to an eventual sprint to the wall. As he reached the top, Spots crashed into him. They both plunged to the ground at the base of the wall, grubs crawling after. Legs tried to get back up the wall and Spots flew upward, bashing into grub after grub. Legs stopped when he reached the top of the wall. Spots was easily fighting away the grubs and Legs stayed still, focused. In one motion, he turned back and left the compound. Spots flew after him, dropping a grub on the ground that he had picked up as he took flight once again.

When Legs and Spots made it back to Asher, Simon, and Digger, all Legs could say was, "They got her." He didn't stop. He kept going. Simon and Asher had to run to catch up, Digger contracted and extended as fast as he could, and Spots flew toward the sea of torches to the north of the compound that the ants had lit to let them know it was time to go.

The group reassembled back at the same hut where they had made their plan earlier.

Inside the hut, Legs was raging; he was sitting in a web of his own making near the ceiling and he was shaking it with his eight powerful legs. The whole hut shook with it. "I will rip the Painting Man apart! I'll wrap him up and hang him from the walls of that place and let the grubs eat him!"

"We'll get her back. I promise." Simon's attempt to reassure Legs was feeble and unconfident.

"No, you won't—I will. It was your plan that got her caught in the first place." The hut seemed like it would come apart from the shaking.

"I'm sorry…" Simon couldn't say any more. He fell to the ground and was crying. He suddenly looked like the ten-year-old that he actually was. There was a crack in the armor now that Asher couldn't see before. Maybe Simon wasn't as strong as he seemed to be, and he shouldn't be. Again… he was only ten years old.

"Yo, Boss," Spots started to say as he moved toward Simon, "We'll all work together or somethin'. It'll be…" Legs sent a web to Spots and pulled him back in a flash.

"I'll do this," Legs said. "Boss, I'm sorry. I didn't mean it." He sidled up to Simon and then pulled his legs underneath his body, lying next to Simon. "Look, I regretted it the second I said that. It wasn't your fault. It wasn't any of our faults. It was the best plan we could come up with and we all knew there was risk to it."

Halfwing entered the hut now.

Legs continued, "Halfwing, Eyes has been caught."

"We gotta do somethin'," Spots said.

"Hush everyone." Halfwing lumbered over to Simon, bent forward, wrapped her good wing around him, then extended it just a little to just touch Legs on his side.

A few silent moments passed. Simon stood up and leaned into

Halfwing who stood with him now and wiped his snotty nose and wet eyes. "I think I know what we need to do, but Halfwing, we're going to need your help."

Simon spoke, not as confident as he had earlier in the day, but the plan made sense. It would be dangerous, but they all thought it would work.

*****

The Painting Man marched with rage into his throne room, dozens of grubs in tow. He turned and stood before his throne. He could not sit; fury pulsing through his being kept him upright and coiled inside, ready to lash out at the first to cross him.

"We were ready! We had them surrounded. We outnumbered them. And yet... you failed to capture the two boys like I commanded! I told you all where they would be and when they would be there. I told you to watch for the spiders and that ladybug. You are worthless!"

One grub stepped forward. "Great leader, they were too fast. We got the girl spider; the others were jus..." and he stopped speaking. The grub was frozen in place.

All the other grubs watched as the Painting Man had slowly raised his hand toward the now silent grub, his face knotted in loathing intent. The Painting Man took slow steps toward the frozen grub. When he reached the grub, he put his raised hand on its head. The grub shimmered and phased out of and into visibility. The other grubs had seen this before and knew what was coming; but they all stayed in place, fearful of possibly being the next. The Painting Man's newest victim was now changing shape and color; no longer the pink-gray of the other grubs, it was now turning a dark brown and changing shape. It grew taller and wider. Its limbs lengthened, and its fingers stretched outward and upward. It's large mandibles spread and grew, then forked into branches upon branches. The grub's head was no longer recognizable as a head at all; instead, it was splintering and vibrating. The grub's legs grew thick and down into the earth. Its skin was cracking all over, but no blood let from its surface. It grew and grew and changed and changed and soon it was clear that it was now a tree.

If Asher were here, he would identify it as a Bigleaf Maple. But he wasn't, and no one cared.

The tree that was once a grub grew to fifty, then eighty feet tall as the Painting Man held his hand on its trunk. It grew leaves which instantly turned brown and dropped. At a hundred feet tall and eight feet wide it stopped growing. Dark spots of blight on its great branches and its trunk appeared and grew until it could no longer hold itself up. In a few seconds it fell, rotted from the inside out. It only crushed a dozen or so other grubs and the Painting Man smirked. The rest of the grubs gave into their instincts and dove, mandibles first, into the great, dead, rotting, tree. It was immediately a feast for the Painting Man's army.

The Painting Man lowered his hand, smirk still malevolently present on his face. He softly said, "At least I was able to make some use of you," as he kicked at the ripped-out roots of the fallen tree. He turned away from the writhing mass of grubs getting their fill and left the room, intent on getting the boys later. He would have what he wanted. He would not stop until he did. His opportunity would come as it always had before.

Day 4 – A Boy Who Needs Help

Little Comets

A light tapping on his forehead woke Asher from a deep sleep. "You were snoring," Lucie said as Asher wiped drool from the side of his mouth and sat up, confused, and still dog-tired. It took a few seconds for him to recognize where he was. He may have gone out to the deck to sleep last night but waking up on the deck was disorienting. His body had technically been resting last night, but his mind was not, and apparently his mind was determining how not-restful he felt in the morning. He wasn't sure what time he came back from the garden-world, but it had to have been well past midnight.

"Did you see any fireballs last night?"

"Fireballs?"

"Your dad said you came out to watch the tau Herculeids. There's no way you'd see any normal shooting stars, but you could have seen some fireballs."

"Oh, yeah… umm… no. No fireballs." Asher had a hard time focusing on Lucie. He couldn't stop thinking about Eyes, how angry Legs was, and how fantastical his life seemed to have become. He couldn't not think about the garden-world.

"You okay, Asher? You look like you saw a ghost."

He shook his head a little and sat more upright. "Yeah. Umm… yeah, I'm okay. I think I'm still just half asleep."

"Hey, can I tell you something?"

"Okay."

"Look, I'm not dumb. I know that something is bothering you and you don't want to talk about it for some reason. It was really upsetting me last night and I yelled at you. I'm sorry."

"No Lucie, I'm sorry. I should tell you about it." He almost did once again, "But I don't totally understand it myself yet. I don't know how to put it in words. If I figure it out, I'll tell you. I promise."

At that moment, they both knew things were okay again. They were still best friends; they were still there for each other. Asher was not really hiding anything from Lucie, and all was almost right in the world… *except for Breitel, and losing their homes, and Simon was in a coma, and Asher's dad was having a hard time handling it all but was trying to hide it, and… okay, maybe all wasn't almost right in the world.*

Asher remembered the plan that he, the Boss, and the bugs came up with last night. He needed to get back to the garden-world as soon as possible this morning. "Hey, let's go tell Mrs. N. about the buildings and Breitel. I want to eat and shower first, can you meet me there in twenty minutes?"

"Sure, I can do that, and you're right, we definitely need to tell Mrs. N. about Breitel because that was super creepy and I'm still kind of scared of him and what the heck was with all those statues because I just don't get it and I don't know if Mrs. N. will know what's going on with those but maybe she'll tell Jenny about them and maybe she'll be able to figure it out or something and maybe she'll find something that will be able to stop Breitel and then we would be able to stay here and not move because it might be cool to be rich and everything but it would be sooo not cool to not live here anymore with me downstairs and you upstairs and we wouldn't have our funnel-phone anymore."

Things were not almost all right in the world, but having Lucie's full, unbridled friendship back and having *that* be right... that was enough for now.

After Lucie left, Asher skipped the shower, quickly changed clothes, ate an expeditious breakfast and was in Mrs. Neighbors' apartment with a full sixteen minutes to tell her about everything that happened in the garden-world before Lucie got there.

Asher tried to tell Mrs. Neighbors all that had happened, rushing through much of it and skipping what he thought might be irrelevant. In the end, they had a couple of minutes to spare and this was when Asher explained the plan.

"So, you see Mrs. N., I need your help to figure out how to keep Lucie busy for the next few hours. I don't know what to tell her."

"I do. Jenny called me this morning and said that she's coming over; there's another property that just sold to Breitel and she wants to share it with us. I'll suggest that Lucie go with her to see it and that I need your help here."

"What will you need my help with?"

"I'll say that I need your help getting to Mrs. Lownsdale's place because I might be able to convince her to buy the building from the Harpers as a back-up."

"Would she do that?"

"Oh no, of course not, but she has the money so Jenny will believe that I would ask her to do so. And she doesn't like me walking that far without help so she'd be happy to have you go with me."

"Mrs. N?"

"Yes, son?"

"Simon... I'm worried that he'll never remember who he is. Will he..."

"Hush son, Lucie and Jenny are both about to..." They heard the door at the bottom of the stairs open, they heard both Jenny's and Lucie's voices, and they tracked them up the stairs.

"Look who I found down in the market," Jenny said pointing to Lucie who did a dramatic curtsy.

"My, you're a ray of sunshine this morning!" Mrs. Neighbors pinched Lucie's cheek, to which she responded with yet another curtsy.

Lucie spoke, "Mrs. N., Asher and I have a lot to tell you and I know I wasn't supposed to tell Jenny that we went and looked at those properties yesterday but I couldn't help it I just told her almost everything we saw yesterday just now and I don't think she's even mad, wait, are you mad Jenny?"

"Not at you, but my grandmother on the other hand..."

"Oh stop it child, they're fine, aren't they?"

"Wait until you hear about the last place they visited yesterday."

Asher and Lucie told Mrs. Neighbors about the loop they took, the statues, the otherwise untouched buildings, and they told her about meeting Breitel. Mrs. Neighbors found their delivery a bit challenging to follow as they popcorned back and forth, interrupting each other and finishing each other's sentences. By the end, Mrs. Neighbors was a bit disturbed; she didn't expect Breitel would ever be any kind of physical threat. She could feel that he wasn't necessarily a nice man, but she believed he was just unfriendly.

"Oh children, we can't have you going out on your own again. That was wrong of me to have you do that."

Jenny spoke now. "Another piece of property has shown up. The sale went through a couple of days ago and my friend at the real estate agency just told me about it last night. I have the address here," she held up a folder, "it's only a couple of blocks west of the place you two saw Breitel yesterday. Based on what you just said, I want to go check it out."

"Asher!" Lucie jumped in, "it's staying in order! Remember? The loop is in chronological order."

"That's right," he said.

Jenny interjected, "Wait, what do you mean?"

"The order in which Breitel bought the properties starts at the church on 13th and goes north and west, then east, then south, then west, and back to... well, here."

Mrs. Neighbors flashed a furtive grimace. "Take Lucie with you. We need to know what's happening there. I need Asher's help this morning. I'm going to go see Mrs. Lownsdale; I think I can convince her to outbid Breitel for this building."

"Grandma, there's no way!"

"I don't care what you think Jenny. I'm going to try."

"Well, at least let me go alone. I don't want to take a child with me." Lucie tensed her jaw at being called "a child." Jenny directed this next part right at Lucie, "It's too dangerous."

"Nonsense. She's smart and capable and she knows what Breitel looks like."

"I'll be careful, and I'll be helpful and besides, you might need me to look in a window if it's high up and you can put me on your shoulders or something like that."

Jenny resigned herself to the fact that she would eventually lose this fight. "Alright, but you do exactly as I tell you the whole time."

*****

Jenny Neighbors was driving, and Lucie was seated next to her. "Lucie, when we get there, you do everything I tell you. If Breitel is there, I want to keep you safe from him."

"Are you going to take a picture of him?" Lucie was pointing to a camera that Jenny had on the floor of the vehicle.

"No, I won't take a picture of him just yet, but I do want a picture of the building and the statue if there is one in there."

Lucie's mind drifted and she bit her thumb out of anxious habit, "Jenny, I'm worried about Asher."

"I know." Jenny lowered her tone, trying to sound sympathetic. "My grandmother told me that you two are struggling with this. How are you?"

"I don't know. I don't want to move. But Asher's mom's garden… it's like Asher needs it. It seems like, I don't know, like he needs the garden to feel better about losing his mom."

"You're probably right, sweetie. No matter what happens, Asher's dad will make sure he's okay. I've known that family for many years and watching Ray take care of himself, Asher, and Simon… and honestly, watching him handle all the necessary things he had to deal with when Lynn died, he's a strong man and strong father. He makes it happen every day, he'll continue to take care of Asher. No matter what."

"I'm still worried. Something's bothering him and he's not talking to me about it."

"Listen sweetie, I'm going to tell you something you might not like to hear. You and Asher are only twelve, and although you're both getting bigger and older, and able to handle more, you're still children. He's learning how to deal with things that are difficult. You know, I'm still learning how to deal with things that are difficult."

"That's what I mean, Jenny. What if he doesn't figure it out?"

"Okay, I'll keep an eye out for him and for Ray."

Silence set in thick, Lucie not knowing what to say.

"Okay?" Jenny pressed.

"Okay." They sat without words for a few more moments. "Thanks."

"Sweetie, all we can do is try to stop Breitel from buying. The only way we're going to do that is to come up with some kind of evidence to prove that he's doing something illegal." Even as she said this, Jenny was unconvinced herself.

Jenny parked her car on 4th Avenue near Chapman Square. It was a slow drive through downtown Portland, but it wasn't even a half-mile from the Harpers' building. They stepped out and Jenny leaned toward Lucie, "Keep me between you and the street. The property is a block away from here. Breitel doesn't know me, but he knows what you look like so if you see him, step behind me and let me know."

"Okay, I promise."

They walked the block quickly before Jenny stopped. "This is it." She was pointing to the bottom floor of a building. The top floor was occupied with apartments, but the bottom floor was obviously vacant. It was dark and there were large windows along the entire face. Brown paper had been placed on the inside of the windows so that passersby could not see into the space, just like the place that Asher and Lucie saw Breitel at the day before. "Do you see Breitel anywhere?"

"No."

Jenny picked up her camera and started taking pictures. As Lucie kept an eye out, she noticed that there was a gap at the top of the brown paper. "Jenny, look!" She pointed up toward the gap.

"Oh... yes, that'll work!" Jenny held her camera as high as she could and snapped a few pictures. "I'll try to get the film developed today. But it probably won't turn out. I didn't use a flash in case he was in there."

"I bet if you put me on your shoulders, I would be able to see in."

"I'm not putting you on my shoulders; people will wonder what we're doing."

"Please, just do it fast. I'll go up and look and then we'll leave right away before anyone sees us."

"People will see us right away."

"Well then, let's do it now, really fast, so we can get going."

Jenny gave in once again and put Lucie on her shoulders, her desire to know what was inside outweighing her sense of good judgment.

"Okay, umm... it's dark in there." Lucie had her face pressed against the glass with her hands blocking the sides of her eyes to keep out as much ambient light as she could. "I can't see much. It's pretty empty. Wait, I see him!"

"Come down now."

"No, he's turned away. He can't see me. He's..." Lucie stopped talking.

Lucie didn't understand what she was witnessing. Breitel was standing shirtless in front of a man who had his eyes shut. The man was just standing still, like he was asleep on his feet. Breitel was slowly waving his hands in front of and around the man. She could see that he was holding little flashlights. No, they weren't flashlights, the light was coming from Breitel's palms. He moved his hands in a smooth, circular pattern all around the man. She could see that the light left trailers behind and she thought that it looked like he was holding little comets. Breitel moved his hands closer and closer to the man's head. He put his hands over the man's ears and the lights crawled into the man's head. His whole head began to glow. The light began to slither back up Breitel's arms and then to his shoulders. It swirled all around Breitel's upper body and left patterns on his skin. The light patterns undulated and glowed brighter with every second that passed.

Suddenly, in an instant, the light flashed so bright that it lit up the entire room.

Lucie climbed down before Jenny was ready for it. Jenny yelped but Lucie put her hands over Jenny's mouth.

Lucie said, "Let's go!" She led them away into Chapman Square to a copse of small trees and bushes. She held Jenny's hand in her own as she put a finger up to her lips. Lucie turned back toward the building. A minute passed and the standing-sleeping man and Breitel stepped out of the building, Breitel now with his shirt and jacket back on. The standing-sleeping man was awake, but he had a blank look on his face; after a few steps out of the building, he sat down on the curb and then... nothing... he did nothing, just sat there with that blank look on his face. Lucie could see past Breitel into the building and in the place where the standing-sleeping man had the light put into his head by Breitel, was an unmistakable, white statue of that very same man. Jenny didn't see the statue; she wasn't ready to be looking for it like Lucie had been.

"Was that Breitel?"

"Yes."

"What else did you see in there?"

"Uhh… just another statue."

"Why is that other man just sitting there like that?"

"I don't know." Lucie wouldn't make any eye contact with Jenny.

"Let's get going. I'd like to get as many pictures as possible of the other properties before we need to get back to my grandmother's."

As they went from property to property with Jenny snapping pictures, Lucie questioned herself. Had she really seen what she saw? Did Breitel just turn a man into a statue? Were all of the other statues once people? It couldn't be, but that was what she had seen. What were the lights? Was it magic? She felt stupid thinking Breitel was using magic. What strange machinations had she just witnessed in that building? She had no answers that did not make her feel unhinged.

The Boss, The First Statue, and The Painting Man

After Lucie and Jenny left Mrs. Neighbors' apartment, Asher went back across the hall, through his apartment, back to the garden on the deck. His father had started his morning much earlier with a visit to Simon and then some extra work at the office. Asher was thankful that he wouldn't have to navigate through his father to get to the deck and the garden. He would only have a couple of hours but that should be enough.

When he showed back up in the garden-world, everyone was ready to go, and he was once again astounded at the capabilities of the bugs, who had built all the weapons, tools, and armor in the last few hours.

"Asher, you're up here with me." Halfwing motioned him over to a small, makeshift, web-made saddle on Legs' back. Digger was in a basket that would be carried by Spots. Pharaoh and Goldy were leading the ants and Simon was on Pharaoh's back in a small web-made saddle of his own. The ants all had clubs with web on one end that attached to stones, or knots of wood. It reminded Asher of medieval flails.

Simon yelled out, "Let's go!" and they were off—fast; there was no wasting time this morning. That, in fact, was part of the plan—attack immediately. Don't give them time to get ready. Be unexpected.

As they started to move forward, Legs stopped by a V-shaped wooden structure. It was half as tall as Legs and just as long. Legs started to crawl all over it. When he crawled down, Asher saw that Legs had built a web-made harness that he then walked right into. He started to move, and the V-shaped structure became an armored plow. Asher thought of the pointed grills on the front of trains, *cowcatchers* they're called. He looked around and saw that several dozen of the ants also had these same V-shaped plows, just a little smaller than the one that Legs was carrying.

Asher felt the wind press against his face from the speed at which Legs was moving. In minutes, they were through the bush that separated the garden from the open area that led to the Painting Man's compound. Legs was not the first out into the open; when they were clear of the brush, Asher saw several columns of quickly-marching ants already halfway into the open space. They were coming from all sides, a true swarming.

"Head toward the southeast corner." Halfwing directed Legs and as he turned, Spots and Pharaoh followed; Goldy kept her direction and they parted from one another. "Legs, climb over at the third torch from the corner, that's the direction they are being held." It was Halfwing's job to sense where Leaf and Eyes were being held captive. She could direct the others where to go, even if she was physically incapable of actually fighting—her role was pivotal if they were to have any chance at success.

As they got closer, more and more grubs lined the top of the wall. Asher was about to witness a battle of enormity; grubs were going to die, ants were going to die. The numbers would be tragic, and Asher suddenly felt a pang of guilt that what they were doing might be wrong. But when would it end if it didn't end today? What would the eventual loss be? What would the eventual tragedy be?

The first ants and their flails made it to the top of the wall and crashing, yelling, and crunching could be heard across the entire face of the compound. Legs needed to avoid as much fighting as possible and just go where Halfwing directed; the ants that preceded them had taken all the attention from the grubs, making it an easy breach. When they got to the wall themselves, Spots flew right over, Pharaoh climbed over, and Legs simply jumped; while in the air, Asher heard him let out a rage-filled growl that turned into a guttural yell. He landed in the middle of a knotted bunch of grubs; he climbed over those he could, and the V-shaped armor plowed through the rest. Legs was stomping on grubs with each step and it shook the saddles that held Asher and Halfwing.

Halfwing reached one hand down to Legs and his rage subsided, the stomping subsided, and he started to move a little quicker now. "Left around the next building. Go along the wall. Right. Straight on to the tallest building." As Halfwing gave these directions, Legs moved faster and faster, Pharaoh and Spots barely keeping up.

Approaching the tall building that Halfwing had directed them toward, Asher saw that this was the largest building in sight, and it appeared to be near the center of the compound. Halfwing directed them to go right over the wall because too many grubs were collected near the entrance to this building. When they got over, there were no grubs in sight; apparently the plan was working, and the grubs were all moving toward the fighting at the wall. As long as the ants kept up the fighting, numbers and skill were on their side; the grubs' mandibles were their only dangerous weapon, otherwise, they were slow and useless. The ants simply had to use their speed to keep away from the mandibles and an occasional club.

Halfwing had stopped directing them. They were inside the largest building now. They stood in a hallway, long in both directions and with no ceiling, an unhindered view of the clouds during the day and the thousands of stars visible at night in the garden-world. "We need to go slow and carefully now. I can't feel rooms, or walls, I can only feel the grubs, Leaf, Eyes, and a few others I can't identify. The Painting Man is in here too."

Simon slid off Pharaoh's back. "Halfwing, which direction will we find Leaf and Eyes?"

"There." She pointed straight to the wall, perpendicular to the hallway they were currently in.

"Digger, it's your turn now. Go get the lay of the land."

"Yes Boss, be right back." He dove into the dirt beneath their feet and was gone in an instant. In under two minutes he was back. They gathered all around as he began to draw a map in the dirt. "It's simple. The other side of this wall is a large, open room. It's empty, I'm not sure what it's for. Right after the room is a hallway that leads to several rooms left and right. We need to go over two more walls to get to the other side of those rooms. That's where Leaf and Eyes are. By the way, they're both okay."

Simon interjected, "So you saw them?"

"Yes. They are in one corner of a large room. They're surrounded by about twenty grubs with clubs."

"What else is in there?" Simon was looking down at Digger's map as he asked this.

"They saw me so I had to leave immediately, but I think I saw more grubs on this side of the room." He pointed to the adjacent corner from where Leaf and Eyes were imprisoned. "There was some kind of wooden structure, maybe a cabinet, in between the two groups of grubs. No ceiling, so we can continue to go right over the walls to get there." Simon was drawing, filling in details on the map based on what Digger was saying.

Legs spoke, "Let's go then. Let's get them. They won't stop us—I promise you that!"

Simon put a hand on his back, "No Legs. We're not quite ready yet. Halfwing, do you sense anything in there we need to know about?"

"Well Boss, I think that Digger is right about the number of grubs. I'm having a difficult time though; the Painting Man feels like he's everywhere in this place, but I sense he is *more* that way." She pointed in the direction of the room with Leaf and Eyes.

"Then we need to be ready. Spots, when we get there, I want you to look for the Painting Man and go right for him; if you can, just knock him out. If he's unconscious he won't be able to direct the grubs."

Asher watched Spots smile with glee and crack his knuckles; Asher wasn't sure, but he thought that Spots probably liked to fight.

"Legs, you go for Leaf and Eyes, plow through the grubs and make a path for them; you should be able to handle that with the wedge," Simon tapped the V-shaped plow harnessed onto Legs. Legs was already massive, four times the size of the largest of the grubs; with the wedge, he would be unstoppable.

Simon continued, "The rest of us will go over, but I want Halfwing and Pharaoh to stay in this last hallway. Halfwing, I want you to be able to focus elsewhere, sense for threats, and warn us if we need to leave. Pharaoh will protect you and get you out if he needs to. I'll go over in the basket with Spots, and Digger can dig his way there. Once we are there, Digger, Asher, and I will go and help whoever needs it. We just need to give Leaf and Eyes a chance to run. Once they're free, we'll all go. If this goes right, we should only be in there a few seconds."

Legs spoke again, "Alright, we're set, let's go!"

Simon responded, "Yes, we're set, let's go."

There was no hesitation as they went over wall after wall—Spots flying, Legs running and jumping—and they entered the final room at the same time. Spots set the basket down just as Digger shot up from the ground like a geyser. Spots could see that the Painting Man was in this room to the right surrounded by even more grubs than Leaf and Eyes were.

Asher slid off Legs' back as he turned left toward the crush of grubs guarding Leaf and Eyes. Legs rushed toward them, his gaze locked on his daughter, Leaf visible in his periphery.

Simon looked left toward Legs as well. He could see that Legs did not need their help; grubs were bouncing off the V-shaped wedge like snow off a snowplow, Legs' mass being the clear advantage. Simon motioned Asher and Digger right toward where they could see Spots charging the Painting Man, flying right over the grubs. The plan was for Simon and Asher to take the grubs down by breaking their mandibles with the flails. Digger would wend through their legs tripping them and then Asher and Simon would strike while they were down. If they kept to the edges, they would be able to keep mostly safe.

With Digger's help, Asher and Simon had taken down two grubs when Asher noticed the grubs weren't fighting back. The Painting Man just stood still, waiting. The grubs were motionless, so he, Digger, and Simon stopped their attack. He looked back toward Legs; Leaf and Eyes were already free and were moving toward the wall to climb back over, their cells demolished by the raging Legs. He looked again toward Spots and the Painting Man; Spots was landing blow after blow and the Painting Man was letting him. The Painting Man stood taking each hit, mostly to the face, as if it weren't even happening at all.

Simon yelled out toward Spots, "Let's go! They're free!" Legs was ready to get Asher and Simon both. Spots stepped back, stupefied, wondering how the Painting Man had not been affected by his pummeling. He turned and flew over the wall.

The Painting Man disappeared; Simon grabbed Asher, "Where is he? Do you see him?" The grubs were now marching out of the room and Legs was calling for them to climb on his back; Digger had already left. The sudden emptiness of the room closed in on Asher; it was now devoid of everyone except for him, Legs, and Simon.

A bright flash momentarily blinded the three of them. Asher could hear Halfwing yelling, brought over by Pharoah, "You must leave now! It's a trap!" Asher's thoughts were tumbling through his mind like white, frothy rapids. *Trap? What? Where? How?* As his vision came back to him, he saw that the Painting Man was now standing right where the flash came from, near the wall next to the cabinet Digger identified earlier. Asher grabbed Simon's arm and pulled him toward Legs. Simon was fixed on the Painting Man now, resisting Asher's pull.

"Come on, let's go!" Legs sent a shot of web toward Asher and Simon. He had them now and he started to run, dragging the two boys behind and with a small hop, the momentum threw the boys onto his back. Simon pulled a small knife from his waist and cut the web. He jumped right off Legs' back and ran toward the Painting Man. Asher grabbed at Legs' head begging him to stop.

Asher heard Halfwing again, "It's a trap, Boss! Come back! We need to leave now!"

Legs stopped as Asher had asked and turned to face Simon and the Painting Man. Simon stood in front of the massive cabinet which Asher now noticed was open. Asher could not see into the cabinet, but whatever it was, it held had Simon completely transfixed. The Painting Man was no more than a few feet from Simon, but he did nothing; he was looking right at Asher with an ominous grin stretched wide. Asher was looking closely at him for the first time now. He had black hair, hanging straight down the sides of his face. He wore a small, brown covering through his mid-section, maybe leather. He wore nothing else, but his skin was covered in black swirl patterns which almost seemed to move over his body. Tattoos? Maybe, but Asher didn't think so. Asher looked again at his face, which also had the swirl patterns, and locked eyes with him. The Painting Man's eyes were filled with malevolence; they were cold, and they were silver.

Asher could hear both Halfwing and Legs calling for him and Simon. Their voices faded as he focused on his brother and the Painting Man. He carefully walked toward Simon; he wanted to grab his hand and try to pull him away. The Painting Man seemed unworried. He was doing nothing—Asher hoped he would continue to do nothing. Closer, closer... he was within reach of Simon now and the Painting Man still stood, staring, not moving, and not speaking, still grinning and still cold.

Reaching for Simon's hand, he now looked away from the Painting Man and into the cabinet. The wooden cabinet was tall and wide, the opened doors revealing its depth. Inside the cabinet was a white statue; that's what Simon was staring at. Everything stopped in Asher's mind. He could see it now. He could see now what Simon saw earlier, what made Simon stop and come this way.

The statue was their mother. Her face was kind. Her arms held together in front of her as if she were holding an invisible baby.

"Do you like it? This was the first one I made here." Asher heard the Painting Man speaking now but kept his gaze on the statue.

"You do seem to be taken with it. Don't you think it's pretty?" The Painting Man's words burned, and Asher couldn't put thoughts together to give any kind of response.

Simon pulled his hand out of Asher's, climbed up into the cabinet and then into the arms of the statue. Asher watched his little brother climb and was now lost for what to do. Simon looked so broken and fragile, laying in his mother's arms, but not really his mother's arms. Asher called to him, but Simon wasn't responding; he was trying to nestle his cheek into the cold stone of the neck of the statue. Asher could see that Simon wanted to be hugged back and was doing all he could to make it happen. Simon was silent, but he was heaving with tightly-held sobs. This hit Asher deeply in his gut; this was wrong, his baby brother didn't deserve this. Asher wanted to tell him that their dad was taking care of him, but he thought that Simon probably wouldn't even hear or understand the words right now.

"You would like it here. I promise. I've been waiting for you to see all of this. I really do think you'll like it." The Painting Man's words were thick and though they sounded welcoming, they felt duplicitous.

Things were clearing in Asher's mind, and one feeling was foremost for him now—fury. He screamed more than spoke, "What do you mean this statue was the first one you made?" Asher's throat went raw with each word hurled at the Painting Man. "No! I don't like it here! I won't like anything you make.

What are you talking about?"

"I can teach you to be great… to do what I do. You are a powerful boy, and you will be more and more powerful as time goes on, but you need someone like me to teach you."

"What are you talking about? I'm not powerful." Asher was beginning to feel that maybe the Painting Man understood something about him that he didn't. He thought about how he still didn't really understand how he could move back and forth between the real world and the garden-world.

"There. That thought you just had. You know you are capable of more, and part of you knows I'm right."

Asher couldn't respond. Could the Painting Man read his thoughts? He looked at Simon again. Was the Painting Man controlling Simon's mind?

"No, I'm not controlling your little brother's mind."

"How did you know?"

"Because I *can* read your thoughts. And I can teach you to read the thoughts of others too."

"No." Asher couldn't think of anything else to say, but he was certain of his "no."

"Are you sure? I can help you reunite with your little brother."

"How did you make this statue?!?!"

"What, this thing?" He moved toward the statue of Asher's mother and put a hand on its foot—Asher's mother's foot. At the touch, the black swirls from the Painting Man's skin flowed onto the statue, briefly dancing all over the surface, then blinked out like a black candle-flame wisping out of existence by a breath.

"Yes, this statue of my mother. How did you make it?"

"Well, this statue is not what it seems. It's a trick, really." Asher listened. "It looks like a statue because it takes the form of its source."

"What do you mean "source"?"

"It's not made from stone."

"Then what's it made from?"

"You're angry with me, aren't you?"

"Yes! Now explain!" Asher glanced up again and saw that Simon had moved his head around to the other side of the statue's neck, the neck of their mother, his body still shuddering with quiet sobbing as he tried to find a more intimate embrace.

"You're angry. You're probably angrier right now than you've ever been, but you know that you will probably be even angrier if I don't give you answers."

"YES! Just give me the answers."

"I am. I need to explain things to you that you'd never understand based on what you already know, so I need to teach you."

"Just tell me. Tell me now!" Asher knew he sounded like he was giving a threat but had no idea how he would back it up.

"Your anger, the anger you're feeling right now. It's powerful. It's limitless. Human emotion is limitless. Human thought is practically limitless. And yet it exists."

"Yeah, so?"

"Do you agree that it exists? Human thought and emotion?"

"Yeah. Again, so?"

"And electricity, and light?"

Asher nodded and tightened his lips.

"Light exists, right?" The Painting Man kept pushing.

"You're talking in circles now and I don't like it."

"If you let light fall onto a dark surface, that surface will absorb the light and it will heat up. Or it might even dry out a

190

worm on a sidewalk."

"What?"

"Electricity is weightless and yet it's powerful enough to gather itself together and strike down trees in the forest on a late summer afternoon."

"Light and electricity are weightless yet powerful. Your thoughts and emotions are powerful. What you think of as *thoughts and emotions,* what humans think of as *thoughts and emotions,* are more than that. They are an energy that flows through a fabric connecting all things. I have the ability to gather the energy of thought and emotion and mold it to my liking and for my purpose, like your scientists and engineers do with batteries and power grids."

"How?"

"I just do."

"How did you make this statue?!"

"I happened upon a person who had more thought and emotion than I had ever seen. I needed it. I was new to this place—you call it Portland—and I needed to establish an anchor." As he said "anchor," he waved toward the statue. "She was in an accident and her thoughts and emotions were going to go up."

Asher felt like he was reliving his mother's death. "What do you mean "go up"?"

"Some call it spirit. They say that a person's spirit goes to heaven. They're right, that's exactly what happens sometimes. Unless someone like me can gather it and use it to create something else. And I created this place."

"So, when my mom died, you gathered up her... her spirit and used it to make this statue? Why?"

"Yes, I didn't use it to *only* make this statue; this statue is just an anchor that holds her energy here. I used it to make everything else you see here. The walls, the floors, the trees, it's all made of the stuff of your mother's thoughts and emotions. I told you, she had more than anyone else I'd ever seen. I believe that's why you are so powerful."

"Why do you keep saying I'm powerful? How do you know?"

"You can do what I can do, only better. You don't need to make anchors."

"No, I can't. Why do you think I can do this?"

"Because you've already done it."

"What? No, I haven't."

"Yes, you did. The day I made this place, you also made a place."

"What place?"

"The garden your friends tend. The moth, and the ladybug. The spiders and the ants. You even made your worm friend, just a few days ago." Asher remembered the earlier visit to the garden-world when Halfwing and Spots said that everything had come from him. They didn't know how; they just knew it had. But something still felt wrong with what the Painting Man was saying.

"No, I didn't. I know that I didn't. You're lying. Why?" He was trying to fight everything the Painting Man was saying but even as he said this, he remembered putting the worm in the tomato box on his last day of school. He felt so warm inside as he covered it with dirt and made sure it was wet. He was feeling great care in that moment.

"You are proving to yourself that I am speaking truth to you. The garden and your bug friends, your worm friend, are what you made, even if you didn't intend to do so."

"Then how did I make them?" Asher thought he might catch

the Painting Man in a provable lie if he kept asking questions.

"When your own thoughts and your emotions are focused on something strongly enough, you become a lens for all that energy around you—it flows through. Your thoughts and emotions, and those of others as well."

"I don't think I understand."

"You saw your mother, in that hole, in the car. In that instant, all of you was focused purely on your mother, you became something that naturally attracted all the thoughts and emotions around you, so much energy that you spontaneously created something to hold it all—the garden."

"Why would I create that?"

"You can answer that yourself, don't you think?" The Painting Man had Asher, and Asher knew he was right.

"I don't... I'm not sure."

"Go ahead. You'll feel better when you accept what I'm saying."

Asher didn't want to give in to the Painting Man, but he felt like he had to face this as well. "My mom's garden. On our deck. That's what I thought about when I saw the accident. I thought of Simon. And Mrs. Neighbors, and J.J. and K.K., and Mr. Harper—they were on the sidewalk below. I thought about all those things just before I passed out. I knew that they were all going to be hurt by it; they all loved... love...my mother and Simon."

The Painting Man stayed silent, but his attention let Asher know that he could keep talking. It was flowing now, all coming together in Asher's mind.

"When I woke up, my dad had come back from the paper and was holding me; he was crying. He kept saying that he would take care of me. We were on the deck in the garden. There were paramedics there. I asked about my mom and Simon and he had to tell me what happened. I didn't know before I passed out."

"You didn't exactly pass out," the Painting Man interrupted. "You were making this place in that moment and it took all of your power to do so. You gathered up all the pain, and all the fear, and all the love, and all the thoughts of all the people around you in the moment you saw your mother's car. All that energy needed to go somewhere, and you created the garden with your bug friends. Your mind and heart had no capacity for anything more than the act of creating, so it felt to you like you passed out, when really, you were just unable to be conscious of anything else at the time."

"Why did I gather all that energy? I wasn't trying."

"Some people are special. They attract it. You might know them as psychics, or empaths, or maybe just people who others find to be unusually caring and inviting. You and your mother are two of the most special in this way."

Asher was getting a handle on this now, or at least, enough of a handle that he wanted to know more. "Why are you telling me all of this?"

"I want you to create more with me. It's difficult for me to create. It's easy for you."

"But why do you want to create these places anyway?"

"I am very old. I don't remember my beginning. I only remember making these places. I need them to live. They eventually run dry and I must then move on and make new places. If I run out of this energy, I will simply end."

This was going down a path that Asher wasn't sure he wanted to follow, but he needed to know more. "How do you know this?"

"I watched it happen to others before me—who were like me."

"I recognize you. You're Breitel, why do you have the statues in those buildings in the real world?"

"Well, yes and no, I use Breitel's body, but I'm not him."

"What do you mean?"

"Breitel, that body at least. I'm… borrowing it. My thoughts and emotions, the stuff that makes me… well, *me*, is using that body. My original body died hundreds of years ago."

"What? So, you've just been stealing other people's bodies? And what about those statues?"

"Each one of those statues is an anchor to help me harness the energy from thoughts and emotions. They act like magnets and anchors at the same time. I use that energy to sustain this place. This is a world, just like what you call the real world. But the real world is held together with gravity and rock. This world is held together by the energy and power of human emotion and thought."

"You called it spirit. You're stealing people's spirits. What happened to the spirit that was in Breitel's body?"

"It's here. Woven into everything you see, just like your mother. Except, he was not nearly as exceptional as your mother."

"I don't want to help you do any of this. No! I won't help you."

"If you did, you could live forever like me. And I wouldn't have to take others' spirits anymore. To be honest, I don't like doing that, I really do feel bad about it every time. Imagine living in a world of your own creation. There is nothing more powerful than that." The Painting Man's eyes were wide and determined, his jaw clenched tight.

"Give me back my brother! I'm done here. I'm done with you." He looked back up at Simon, who was unmoved and still shuddering with silent weeping.

The Painting Man laughed deeply, "Oh, poor child. I don't have your brother. I'm not holding him here. This, that you see... him, curled in the arms of this statue, that's his own doing, not mine."

"Fine, then I'll take him myself."

"I don't recommend that, you risk losing him forever."

"How?" Asher had started to climb the statue and stopped.

"He still doesn't remember who he is. His recognition of your mother is only an emotion. He felt comfort, loss, love, and protection when he saw the statue, but he didn't have any actual recognition of who she was."

"I'm going to take him anyway."

"If you do, you risk breaking this last strand of connection between them. He may not be able to handle another separation. You'll lose him forever. He'll be stuck here, unable to return to his body. Eventually, he will wither away into nothing as his energy slowly loses the strength to hold itself together in this form."

Asher's anger turned to fear, and his chin trembled. His throat tightened, and his face was hot. Tears pooled in the corners of his eyes.

"He'll be safe here. I'll make sure of it." Asher immediately thought that his version of *safe* was probably different than the Painting Man's version of *safe*.

"Why would you help me? You obviously don't care about anyone but yourself."

"Well, I care about convincing you to help me. Maybe together, we can help him remember who he is."

"Can you do that?"

"Will you help me?"

"I… I can't." Asher said, looking down. He wiped his runny nose and wet cheeks. "If I'm as powerful as you say, I'll figure out a way to get him back." He turned and ran toward Legs, who was waiting at the base of the wall.

When he got to Legs, he jumped up on Legs' back and Legs tore through the entire compound, everyone in tow. It was mere minutes until they were all back at the garden: Legs, Eyes, Spots, Digger, Halfwing, and Asher all in the small hut where the map lay on the table.

"I'm glad you're not hurt. Halfwing wouldn't let me get you; she told me to stay by the wall and let you go to the Paining Man." Legs sounded remorseful.

"He didn't hurt me," said Asher.

"I could tell that he only wanted to talk. I can feel intent and he did not intend you any harm," Halfwing saying this more to console Legs than she did to explain it to Asher.

Spots spoke, "I *intended* that whackadoo some harm but nothin' doin'. He took every punch and just kept smilin' at me. He's somethin', I don't know what he is… but he's somethin'.'"

Halfwing came over to Asher and wrapped her wings around him. "Let it out child." Asher did. He crumbled in her arms and wings, burying his face into her. A few minutes passed, and he was able to gather himself together.

"Tell us child, what happened when you went to the Painting Man?"

"Why do you call him the Painting Man?"

Legs answered the question, standing next to Eyes, closely and protectively, "a long time ago, when we first arrived here, Eyes and

I were out scouting things, and we were up in a treetop. We could see his compound, it wasn't so big then. He was walking along the wall on the outside and he was waving his hands around slowly. Light was coming from his hands and it left dark swirls all over the walls, like the ones you could see on his skin. It looked like he was painting. The swirl patterns moved all over the walls then faded out."

Eyes continued, "We watched him. We went every day. He did the same thing and his place kept getting bigger and bigger and he would 'paint' those swirl patterns all over everything. We didn't really understand what he was doing but he always had those grubs around and they had weapons. It didn't look too friendly, so we kept a distance."

Halfwing prodded again, "What happened in there with the Boss and the Painting Man?"

Asher squeezed his eyes in frustration, not knowing how to provide a clear answer, "Umm…it's hard to explain. He says I made you, and he made that place where he is. In the big wooden cabinet… it's a statue of my mom. The Boss climbed up into the arms of the statue."

"That's kinda weird," said Spots, "did the Paintin' Man make him do it or somethin'?"

"No. I have to tell you all something." Asher paused, thinking of the right words.

They waited for Asher to continue.

"The Boss, he's more than the Boss. He's… umm… my brother. His name is Simon."

"Ohh… dear child, why didn't you tell us?" Motherly concern enveloped Halfwing's words.

"I didn't know what would happen. He didn't recognize me,

and I didn't know what to do. I thought that if he didn't recognize me, then he would just think I'm crazy if I tried to tell him he was my brother."

"So, is he still there?" Digger had been quiet, but his concern and fear were palpable, and he finally had to give in and ask. "Is he still sitting in the statue's arms? Will he be safe there?"

"Yes. I believe so. The Painting Man wants me to go with him. To make more places like his compound. He won't hurt Simon because he wants my help."

"Well, that's troubling." Digger sidled up to Asher and leaned on his shoulder, an attempt at comforting.

"He wants me to gather more… umm… he says that I can gather people's emotions and thoughts, that it's a kind of energy I can control. He wants me to gather thoughts and feelings from people and then build more of this world or more worlds like this. I don't trust what he says; it seems like he's telling the truth, but I think there's more. But I am sure that when *he* does it, he hurts people. There are these statues where I come from that look like the one of my mom. I think they were people. It's no different than killing people."

"We must stop him," determination poured out of Halfwing with these words. "He will be headed for our garden soon."

They all looked to Asher. The realization that the Boss was Asher's little brother and was now in the keep of the Painting Man—and in danger—hung thick in the small hut.

"I don't know what to do. I'm not like Simon. He's good at strategy. He always has been. I like facts and knowledge. I don't know how to get him back… to save him."

Legs skittered forward to the middle of the hut and crawled up on the table. "The Painting Man took my daughter. We may have gotten her back, but I'm not done with him. Now that he has the Bo… Simon, I can't let that stand. Asher, I promise you, we will all work together to get Simon back and stop the Painting Man."

Halfwing stood, looking on with pride at Legs, "We promise."

"You bet'chyer a…"

"SPOTS!" Halfwing interrupted.

"I mean, you bet'chyer heinie we promise!"

Digger inched over next to Asher. "I don't know why I feel this way Asher, but I feel like it's my job to protect you and the Boss… I mean, Simon. There's only one thing I want, it's to get Simon back and stop the Painting Man from ever hurting either of you again." Digger wended his way around Asher's legs, and it felt to Asher like a hug. "We promise."

Eyes spoke now, "Simon and you and everyone in this room saved me and Leaf. I promise too. And we've learned a few things from the Boss. I think we can get them back if we work together."

"Thanks everyone," Asher couldn't hide the quivering of his chin or help but push his bottom lip out as he spoke, a telltale sign of his youth, "I need to get back to the real-world. They're probably waiting for me and there's some pretty important stuff happening there too."

Asher Tells Lucie

Back in Mrs. Neighbors' apartment, Asher told her all about what just happened, the clash of ants and grubs at the compound wall, Halfwing's guidance and Digger finding Eyes and Leaf, that Breitel was the Painting Man, Breitel's invitation, the statue of his mother and Simon climbing onto it, now trapped, and the last moment in the hut where the bugs pledged their determination and allegiance to Asher and Simon.

"Listen son, it sounds to me like you have a formidable set of friends who will get Simon back for you."

"Yeah, but I want to help. I can't not help."

"That's what I thought. If you're going to help, you will need to do it tonight so that you can camp out on your deck again."

"Will you come with me?"

"I don't know how to, son."

"The Painting Man says I'm powerful, more powerful than him. I think I could take you with me if I tried hard enough." Asher's eyes were pleading with her...

"What would I do? I'm old and slow."

"You can ride on Legs' back. When we get there, you can do that thing where you feel people and you can tell us where to go. You know, Halfwing can do that, too."

"Really? That's interesting."

"It'll be helpful, because we can split up and still have both groups guided by someone."

"Okay, I'll help. To be truthful with you child, I had hoped there was a way I could go there. It sounds extraordinary. Jenny and Lucie are on their way up the stairs."

Jenny and Lucie soon walked into Mrs. Neighbors' apartment. "My pager went off grandma; may I use your phone?"

"Sure thing, sweetheart. You know where it is."

As Jenny stepped into the kitchen, Lucie started talking. "There's another statue and I saw Breitel there and… umm… uhh… that's it. We drove around and took pictures of the other properties after we looked at that one."

Mrs. Neighbors narrowed her eyes and touched Lucie's hand. Lucie shot a quick glance at Mrs. Neighbors. Mrs. Neighbors' gaze felt like she was peering into her soul. Lucie could tell that Mrs. Neighbors knew she was hiding something; she was glad Mrs. Neighbors didn't say anything.

Jenny returned. "I've got to go to the station. There's a story I need to cover with Matt. We need to have it ready for the five o'clock. I'm going to talk to a lawyer friend of mine tonight. Maybe he's in breach of contract if he's not remodeling the buildings. It's a stretch, but it's all I can think of right now."

"Go ahead, dear. I'll keep an eye on the children and I won't let them go out there alone again, I promise." Jenny bent and gave her grandmother a kiss on the cheek and was out the door.

"Asher, why don't you and Lucie go check on the garden. Some of those plants need watering at least twice a day when the sun is out like this."

"Uhh… alright. But…" Asher looked quizzically at Mrs. Neighbors, who just smiled at him and shooed them out the door.

Across the hall and on the deck, Asher started to grab the

watering can and a hose.

Lucie grabbed his arm. She held it firmly and looked at him with a hard gaze. She took a deep breath and said, "Asher, I need to tell you something."

"Okay."

"You need to promise me you'll listen."

"Okay."

"And don't tell me I'm wrong, or that I don't know what I'm talking about, or I'm imagining things."

"Okay."

"Promise?"

"Promise."

"Promise?!?!" She held tighter and steeled her stare.

"Geez, I promise." Asher thought to himself that no matter what she had to say, she'd never understand what he, himself, had seen.

"Okay. Well. Umm. Uhh."

"Just sa…"

"SHUT UP! Don't interrupt; just give me a second."

"Sorr…"

"I said shut up and listen!"

Asher did the zip-my-lips-and-throw-away-the-key motion.

"Well. Okay… I'm just going to say it. Breitel is some kind of warlock or magician or something weird and I know that sounds like I'm crazy and I know it sounds like I have to be wrong but I know what I saw and I saw him create light out of his hands and he had his shirt off and it was weird and he had all these tattoo things all over his body except they kept moving around his body so it's like they were floating tattoos or something and then there was this other guy and he looked like he was sleeping while he was standing and Breitel was making all these weird lights come out of his hands and he kept waving his hands around like he was dancing or something and then he put the lights into the man's head and then the man became a statue. Except… the man was also still there. He came out of the building and sat down. I think he's now one of those disconnects Jenny was talking about on the news last night."

"Did Jenny…"

"I said DON'T tell me… wait. What were you going to say?"

Asher was a little afraid to speak again but treading lightly, he said, "Did Jenny see this too?"

"No, but I promise you that I'm…"

"I BELIEVE YOU!"

She jumped and hugged him. "Thank you. You don't know how much that means to me because I didn't even believe it myself I just kept telling myself I must be crazy or maybe I was hallucinating but I know I saw it."

"Come here." Asher pulled her over to the spot on the floor of the deck by the Romas. "Hold my hands, close your eyes, and listen to me. Listen to everything I'm about to say."

"What are we doing?"

"It's kind of hard to explain. I want to just show you."

Lucie followed his lead, closed her eyes, held his hands, and listened.

Asher started, "Take a deep breath through your nose and smell the plants. Ignore the sounds from the street below and just listen to the wind and leaves. Think about this garden. There are tomato plants, and onion, and oregano. There's an earthworm I put in this box a few days ago. Imagine it moving through the dirt in this garden."

Asher was concentrating on gathering Lucie's thoughts and feelings as she listened to his words. He was trying to build a connection so he could take her with him to the garden-world.

"There are spiders in this garden; the moths visit at night under the moonlight. I think there might even be a ladybug who eats the aphids. Think about that ladybug, and think about the spiders, they take care of this garden just as much as I do. They care for it."

Asher could feel something. He didn't know if Lucie could feel it too.

"Think about the smells you're smelling. The spiders and the ladybug. The earthworm."

Asher started to take himself to the garden-world. He felt himself going and he felt that the connection he tried to build was there, and it was strong.

As he felt the spinning and swirling, he could feel that he had to hold the connection stronger. The spinning and swirling, twirling of blackness and lightness all at once felt more sluggish while dragging another through it.

He crashed to his side onto dry and dusty dirt. His hands hurt. They were holding onto Lucie's tightly.

"Ouch, Asher, let go." He did. "Wait… what happened. Did you hypnotize me?"

"No."

"AAAAAAAHHHHHHHHHHHH!!!" Her screech pierced into his dizzied brain and it started pounding.

"Whoa there! Whatcha got there with ya, Asher?"

"What? Huh? Asher, that's a talking ladybug! But it's a man! It's a manbug! AAAAAAHHHHHHHHHH, A MONSTER SPIDER!!!"

Eyes had come around the side of the hut. Lucie turned around to run but saw Legs coming from the other direction. She turned back to Asher, who then gripped her shoulders.

"They're my friends. They're my friends. They're my friends." This stopped Lucie, who was still hyperventilating.

"It's okay. We're safe here. This is what I wanted to show you."

"Uhh… where are we?"

"I can come here, and I brought you here."

"How?"

"Uhh… I guess with my mind," Asher said.

"I don't understand. No, no. I'm hallucinating. This is a dream. It's not real."

She closed her eyes, counted to ten, opened them again and saw Spots' wide-grinned face about three inches from her own.

"Nope—it's real," Spots said with glee as he laughed at her.

Asher spoke to her again, "I wanted to show you this to explain what you saw."

"What are you talking about?"

"The magic you said that Breitel had."

"Oh… you knew? Wait! How did you know?"

"I just found out."

"How? How did you just find out? You weren't with me and still, what is this place?"

"I know that Breitel is magic because Breitel is here too."

Asher went on to explain everything to Lucie. The rest of the bugs had gathered around, and Asher made introductions as he told the stories of what he'd already experienced here in the garden-world. He explained his own abilities according to what Breitel had told him. He explained Breitel's intent and invitation.

"So, you're magic?"

207

"I guess, sort of."

"And Simon is really here?" Lucie was drowning in her confusion; it was too much to take in.

"Yes."

"And we're going to go save him?" Lucie asked.

"Tonight."

"How?"

"We're here to make a plan. We don't have much time left. We'll need to start the plan, let the bugs finish it, and then meet them back here tonight."

"How are we going to do that?"

"You'll need to go camping on my deck with me tonight."

"Okay, my parents will let me, I'm pretty sure. I just need to get my chores done first." Lucie was coming around now.

Asher turned to the bugs, "I don't have a plan, but I do have one idea."

Legs spoke, "Let's hear it."

"Simon needs to be pulled away from the statue safely, it's pretty high." He turned to the two spiders, "Do you two know how to make web-nets like the deinopis spider?"

"We know how to make nets, but we don't know what a deinopis is," Eyes clarified.

"If you know how to make nets, that'll be good enough."

Within a few minutes of working together, they had roughed out enough of a plan that Asher and Lucie could leave, and the bugs could finish up.

Asher and Lucie would be back, later that evening.

Derek Rey

The Man on the News

Ray came back from the Oregonian office around 5:30. It had given Asher and Lucie enough time to calm down, talk out their plans for the rest of the evening, and briefly visit Mrs. Neighbors to get her caught up as well.

"Hi, Dad." Asher jumped up and eagerly gave Ray a hug.

"Well hi there, kiddo. Lucie, you should hang out more often, Asher's hardly ever in this good of a mood."

"Okay Mr. Jakes, happy to."

"Are you joining Asher, Mrs. Neighbors, and me for dinner down at J.J.'s?"

"Yes, Mr. Jakes."

"Do your parents know?"

"Yes, Mr. Jakes. They said they were going to go out on a date-night. I think they were happy to be rid of me."

"Alright then. Why don't you two go and get Mrs. Neighbors? Head on down and I'll catch up after a quick change."

"Okay Dad." Asher and Lucie hopped up and went.

In a few minutes, the four of them were headed into J.J.'s. Asher and Ray both bent down to give a quick rub of the back to the black-and-grey tabby which had become ever-present near J.J.'s. J.J.'s food had apparently garnered some inter-species adoration (and why not?) since it was "sooooo delicious!" ("Sooooo delicious" was what Lucie said at every one of J.J.'s meals.)

In the middle of eating the special, turkey pot pie, Lucie kicked

Asher's ankle under the table. He looked over at her and her face was ashen, wide eyes darting between the television and Asher.

When Asher looked up to the television, he saw Jenny Neighbors.

> "...tell us Matthew. Where are we now with the continuing story of the disconnects?"
>
> "Well Jenny, I'm reporting from Chapman Square. We arrived earlier today to the site just in time to see an ambulance take what appeared to be another disconnected individual up to OHSU. We'll run a few seconds of that footage now."
>
> Red and white lights were flashing on the side of a nearby building as a man on a gurney was loaded into an ambulance. A quick zoom gave a brief glimpse of the man's face.
>
> "If you look right behind me here to the building across from Chapman Square, the one with the brown paper covering the windows and the apartments up above, you see just where the man was found. He was sitting on the sidewalk, in that state of disconnect we have become all too familiar with."
>
> "Any word from OHSU?"
>
> "Yes, we spoke briefly to Dr. Paul Britton, and he stated that there has been zero progress in uncovering the cause or any kind of treatment. But he has also reassured us that this still appears to be non-communicable. The disconnect discovered yesterday near 1st Avenue, and this one, brings the total to forty-five."
>
> "Well Matthew, this is certainly heartrending for the

*Portland public and tragic for the families of the victims.
Do you have anything you can add at this time that would
help to reassure our viewers?"*

*"Only that Dr. Britton assures us that OHSU and
the CDC have a full-time, dedicated team. They have us on
speed dial and will be alerting the public to any news of note
without hesitation."*

*"Pass our thanks on to Dr. Britton and the team next
time you speak with them."*

*"I will. Reporting for KCMW, this has been Matthew
Maxwell."*

Ray was ordering milkshakes for the table when the news cast
ended. Lucie leaned over to Asher and whispered in his ear,
"That's the man. The one that Breitel put the light into and then
made a statue of him."

The two were stunned and continued stealing glances at one
another with concern and fear.

Ray tapped Asher on the shoulder, "Hey kiddo, I asked if you
wanted malt again."

"Sorry Dad, I was just... umm... thinking."

"Well, do you?"

"Do I what?"

"Do you want malt in your shake again?"

"Oh, yes... no, wait... what kind of shake is it?"

"The peach and strawberry are all gone so I got you peanut
butter."

"In that case, yes. Malt please."

K.K. took down a final quick scribble and headed back.

Earlier in the day, Asher, Lucie, and Mrs. Neighbors had worked out that Mrs. Neighbors would hurry dinner along under the pretext of her "hip acting up." It worked better than expected. They also got Ray's permission to spend the night on the deck again. Mrs. Neighbors would be with them, hoping to see a fireball light up the Portland sky—she missed the days when you could see stars from the Park Blocks. Now the city lights were just too bright.

Ray stayed back to help K.K. and J.J. close up the diner and to talk. Even he needed a little friendship right now; J.J. and he were solid friends and had become closer over the last year.

For Asher to bring Mrs. Neighbors into the garden-world, he would need Lucie's help in bringing one of Mrs. Neighbors' rocking chairs from her apartment over to the deck and set it up so she would be comfortable.

Gee, So Furious

Ray entered the apartment and headed to the sliding glass door that led to the deck. He opened it and stepped out to check on his son and guests. He was about to ask if they had seen anything good from the meteor shower but saw that they were all asleep. Even Mrs. Neighbors had nodded off in her little rocking chair. Asher and Lucie must have brought it over for her. He felt gratitude for how Asher and Lucie were turning into such wonderful human beings.

He bent down and pulled the sleeping bags close around Asher's and Lucie's chins. He then stepped back into the apartment to grab a blanket for Mrs. Neighbors. After reassuring himself that they would be okay out on the deck that evening (after all, the weather report said it would be a comfortable, dry night), he grabbed a blanket and pillow for himself and laid down on the couch in the living room to go to sleep within earshot of the three on the deck.

In the garden-world, Asher and Lucie were getting caught up on the plan as Mrs. Neighbors was finding her footing. Even though she was expecting much of what she saw based on what Asher had told her, being here was still disorienting and awe-inspiring all at once.

As new as this place was to Mrs. Neighbors, there was something that felt so familiar about everything and everyone.

Legs appeared to be in charge, "Eyes and I went back with Digger, we found more statues. They're all over the place. Eyes and Leaf have been making maps for everyone who will be leading patrols of ants and also for those of us going straight to find the Boss."

Legs continued with the plan, explaining that Mrs. Neighbors would be on his back as she guided Legs and their party toward Simon; Asher and Lucie would be there as well. Halfwing would be in the basket carried by Spots and those two would survey the work of the ants who would be going around and pulling down the rest of the statues and destroying them. This would also allow Spots and Halfwing to see any dangers or vulnerabilities during the execution of the plan. They would once again be relying on numbers. As long as the onslaught continued all around the compound, Legs, Digger, Eyes, Mrs. Neighbors, Asher, and Lucie should be able to get Simon out. The only worry was that they still didn't know how powerful the Painting Man really was. Spots didn't even leave a scratch. Could Legs do anything to him if it came to that? Asher's plan to have Eyes use a deinopis-inspired net while he, Lucie, and Digger created a distraction would have to be the key.

Speeding through the treetops, Asher looked over at Mrs. Neighbors perched on Legs' back, Digger curled up right behind her. He nudged Lucie; they were both on Eyes' back. Lucie looked and saw what Asher could see; Mrs. Neighbors had a beaming look of delight as her hair trailed in the wind, Legs' speed even greater than it had been earlier that day. Lucie could feel her heart beating so fast and strong that the pulse went through her whole body.

As they all approached the compound, Spots flew north around the far side toward the river so that he and Halfwing could do the initial survey. Legs was headed straight to the section of the wall where he knew he wanted to jump. The wedge harnessed around him would provide protection from whatever was on the other side.

The jump was sudden and powerful, and Mrs. Neighbors was thankful that the web-built saddle and straps holding her in place were strong; she was even more grateful that Digger had wrapped himself around her in a protective embrace. They landed and then she heard the thud of Eyes' landing with Asher and Lucie immediately to their side.

Asher yelled over to Mrs. Neighbors, "Mrs. N! Can you feel where Simon is? Can you feel where the Painting Man… Breitel is?"

"Yes, they are both that way!" she yelled back. The sound of crashing and crunching had just begun; the ants led by Goldy, Pharaoh, and Leaf, with extra guidance from Spots and Halfwing, were quickly getting to work on the grub's defenses and the statues.

Asher yelled over at Legs, "You go that way," pointing north along a row of small buildings, "and Eyes, Lucie, and I will go this way," pointing south along the compound wall which led to two larger buildings. "We'll meet back here in two minutes."

On that command, they split up. The plan was taking form now. Legs was covering as much surface as he could with sticky webbing heading north, covering the small buildings, and Eyes was doing the same going south. When they met back, Eyes climbed the compound wall and walked along until Asher and Lucie had each grabbed a torch. Eyes came back to the ground. Lucie jumped off Eyes' back and climbed up with Mrs. Neighbors onto Legs' back. Legs and Eyes retraced their steps where they had laid webbing, and Asher and Lucie used the torches to light the webbing every few feet, meeting back where they started one more time. The webbing burned briefly, but also brightly and hot—hot enough to catch some of the buildings and wall on fire. The intent was to frighten the grubs who instinctively burrow or run from heat and fire, a factoid Asher had learned from a documentary about Amazonian villages he had watched with his father some years back.

Lucie climbed back onto Eyes and Asher said, "Okay! It's time! Let's go in!"

They moved in the direction in which Mrs. Neighbors had indicated Simon and the Painting Man would be. Asher could see that it was the same place as earlier that day. Apparently, the Painting Man wasn't trying to make this difficult.

As Eyes was jumping over walls, Asher could see Spots and Halfwing in the distance. They were working hard at directing the ants so that they could avoid as many grubs as possible while finding statues to destroy.

They got to the room with the cabinet and the Painting Man, except the Painting Man wasn't there as Mrs. Neighbors had said. The doors to the cabinet were open; the statue and Simon were clearly visible. A black-and-grey tabby cat sat in the cabinet at the foot of the statue. The stripes on its body turned to swirls and it began to grow and grow, and it became the Painting Man. The black marks on his body were pulsating and writhing. There were no grubs in the room. Digger slid off Legs' back. Legs stayed back with Mrs. Neighbors for the moment. Asher, too, slid off Eyes' back. Lucie's job was to stay on Eyes' back for now, ready.

Asher walked up to the Painting Man. "I'm back. I'm here to get my brother."

"That might be what you want to do, but don't you remember? If you do that, you could lose him forever."

"I'm not worried about that. He'll be fine. We both will be fine."

"Asher, come back!" Mrs. Neighbors suddenly started screaming.

The room filled with an exploding cloud of dust. Grubs were shooting up through the dirt. They had been lying in wait.

"Asher!" Mrs. Neighbors yelled again, "I couldn't feel them; there were too many, I didn't recognize them!"

Her words were drowned by the noise of the scrambling grubs. Asher covered his nose and mouth, the dirt in the air making it hard to breathe. He was looking for a way out. He felt strong arms grip him. Two grubs had grabbed him, each holding onto an arm. They put him in a cage made of thick, fresh-cut sticks, still green.

Legs asked Mrs. Neighbors to slide from his back and she did. He rushed through the cloud, the wedge blasting through mobs of grubs. As he hit the cage, it didn't break. The Painting Man had learned. The previous cells that Legs had demolished so easily were of old, dry wood. This new one was of green, wet, thicker wood. It would have to be cut open. Legs was stunned by the ineffectual crash. He gathered his wits and crawled out of the harness that held the wedge. Filled with rage, no longer fully in control, he turned to the Painting Man and charged. He was easily three times the mass of the Painting Man. He was going full speed as he crashed, headfirst, right into the Painting Man's midsection, then fell to the ground, crumpled in a heap, the Painting Man unmoved and unblemished.

Asher saw this and looked over to Eyes, who was calling for her father to get up. The grubs had started to split and charge at each of them. Asher yelled out as loud as he could. "Eyes! Digger! Lucie! Do it now!"

Digger dove into the ground. Eyes sent a bit of webbing to Mrs. Neighbors, gathered her up, and put her atop one of the walls, using webbing to hold her in place so that none of the grubs could get to her. With Lucie still on her back, Eyes ran in concentric circles and then diagonal lines over the heads of the grubs, moving too fast for any of them to grab hold of her. She was laying sticky webbing over the top of and in between them. As they tried to get away or remove the web, it stuck to them more tightly. She was fast, and she finished several circles and lines faster than Asher would ever have expected. Eyes then went to the wall nearby the cabinet that held the statue of Asher's mother. She sprayed sticky web onto the wall and Lucie quickly jumped off and lit it.

Once the fire was lit, the grubs all moved in the opposite direction; the web that Eyes had laid down on them was trapping them in place. The more they struggled, the tighter it got. Soon, all the grubs were stuck to each other, immobilized in the center of the room.

Digger had been digging more holes beneath the grubs. Soon, some of the grubs were falling into his holes, pulling the others down like weights in a fishing net.

This part of the plan was complete. They were expecting a battalion of grubs protecting the Painting Man and Simon; they just didn't expect them to come up from the ground. The grubs were no longer an obstacle, and fire was keeping more grubs from coming this direction. It was now only the Painting Man who stood between them and Simon.

Asher called out to the Painting Man. "Hey, Breitel! We're going to win! You know that?"

The Painting Man turned and laughed at Asher, "You're the one in the cage. Just because you've taken care of the grubs, you now think you're going to win? I don't need them! They're just here to do the work I don't want to do. I'm still more powerful than all of you."

"Are you sure?" As Asher was talking with Breitel, Lucie was pulling out a web-made net from under the saddle on Eyes' back.

"I have so much energy anchored here. This statue of your mother is only the beginning."

"Then why can't you read my mind? You'd know I was right if you could read my mind."

The Painting Man was about to speak, then stopped. He was now startled, panic creeping into his eyes and voice. "What have you done?"

"You can't read my mind. Can you?"

"WHAT HAVE YOU DONE?" The Painting Man squeezed his eyes shut, put his hands over his ears and shook his head. "What have you done? I can't hear your thoughts anymore.

"You thought you could convince me to join you, but you didn't realize you would tell me too much while you were trying to do so. While we've been fighting in here, ants have been destroying the other statues. You said they were anchors that held your energy here, right? And that energy was your source for power and your existence?"

"No… NO!"

"So, what exactly happens if your anchors are broken?

Wouldn't you have less power?"

In that moment, Spots crashed into the Painting Man from Behind, he and Halfwing appearing over the wall a moment before. The Painting Man fell to the ground, stunned. He shook his head and got back up; he ran as fast as he could toward Simon and the statue. The Painting Man got a hand on the foot of the statue of Lynn Jakes. Dark swirls suddenly appeared all over the statue and flowed onto the Painting Man's hand, then arm, and then his entire body.

As Spots came down on the Painting Man once more, his blows did nothing… the Painting Man was filling himself with energy and power.

The Painting Man turned to Spots, stared at him, and sent a guttural yell toward Spots. The yell faded and turned into a flowing blackness, eating all light that passed through. The flowing blackness was dense and brutal as it met Spots' chest. Spots froze in place, but only for the briefest of moments; then, as if there was a silent explosion, he was lifted off the ground and sent backward across the room, crashing to the ground then rolling into the far wall, stopping with a dense thud.

Kaleidoscopic black swirls danced over the Painting Man's skin as he slowly walked toward Asher. Spots and Legs were both unconscious, Digger was continuing his assault on the grubs from beneath, Eyes had moved as far from the Painting Man as she could, defensively hiding Lucie, Mrs. Neighbors, and Halfwing behind her.

The Painting Man was now in front of Asher, and Asher could see that the black swirls are even dancing on the whites of the Painting Man's eyes. The Painting Man held one hand in front of Asher's face. Black swirls slowly flowed from the center of his palm toward Asher. Asher stepped back but had nowhere to go. The swirls found their way to Asher and enveloped Asher's entire head. He was lifted off his feet and then floated back toward the Painting Man. In a second, the Painting Man had the top of Asher's head in his hand.

As Asher saw the swirls get close to his face, and then surround his head, he felt nothing physically, but soon lost control of his thoughts. His life, his memories, were spinning in front of his mind's eye like a tornado of remembered moments and knowledge. He had no control over this. He realized that the Painting Man was mining his memories… and he had no choice in the matter. Suddenly, one image shot forth with enough force that it felt like his brain had been tackled from the inside.

The Painting Man let go of Asher. A corner of his mouth turned upward as his eyes narrowed to slits. He turned away from Asher and started toward the grubs.

Eyes had put Lucie and Halfwing with Mrs. Neighbors on top of the wall, away from most of the danger.

Lucie was none too happy, "Why'd you put me up here? I can help!"

"Asher made me promise to keep you safe. He told me to get you out of harm's way if things got too dangerous." Eyes jumped down and turned toward Asher and the Painting Man ignoring that Lucie was yelling at her. Eyes moved toward the Painting Man carefully, ready to spring, but not sure if she should, not sure what to do at all.

The Painting Man got to the grubs that were bound by sticky webbing, falling into pits created by Digger, and laid one hand on one of the stuck grubs. Black swirls erupted from his whole arm and spread rapidly across the grubs and the webbing.

Asher realized what was happening, knowing the particular memory the Painting Man pulled from his mind, and he yelled toward Eyes.

Eyes could hear Asher, but she didn't understand. "Gee so furious! Gee so furious!" she heard him yell.

"What?" she yelled back.

"Gee so furious! GEE SO FURIOUS!!"

Spots was conscious again. He crawled his way over to Legs and shook him awake.

"GEE SO FURIOUS!"

Legs was able to find Digger and bring him above ground with a tapping of one of his heavily-armored legs right above where Digger was digging. All three of them ready to attack, they began a low and slow movement around the wriggling and writhing grubs. The black swirls that were dancing on the webbing and the skin of the grubs seemed to be causing the grubs to convulse.

"GEE SO FURIOUS!" They, too, could hear Asher but didn't understand him.

All at once, webbing turned to dust and the grubs started crawling out of the holes—except, they weren't grubs anymore.

"GEE SO FURIOUS!"

They had become yellow in color. Their skin was banded, like an earthworm's. They now had long, thin mandibles, a tiny head, and a large body. Lucie could see them, and she thought they looked like yellow lightbulbs with legs.

"GEE SO FURIOUS!"

Spots was having none of this. He leaped forward and brought his fist back, ready to land his heaviest blow. One of the used-to-be-grubs found its way in between Spots and the Painting Man, who simply stood with his crooked smile, unmoving. Spots' fist landed squarely in the center of the used-to-be-grubs' abdomen. It immediately pinched Spots with its long, thin mandibles.

"GEE SO FURIOUS!"

"Nah, kid! Don't worry 'bout it," Spots said to Asher, "This thing ain't that strong. His pinch doesn't even hurt."

"No Spots! It's Gee so furious!" Spots heard Asher say as he gripped a mandible in each of his thick, calloused hands.

"I got this, kid!"

"No Spots, it's an exploding Malaysian termite! It's a trap!"

As Spots pulled the mandibles apart, the used-to-be-grub exploded, warm yellow liquid covering Spots' hands, arms, chest, and face. In a second, the liquid hardened, and Spots was frozen.

The used-to-be-grubs—now termites—swarmed the others, and as they grabbed with their mandibles, they exploded, sending yellow liquid over anything and anyone nearby. In seconds, Eyes, Digger, Legs, and even more of Spots, were all frozen in the hardened, yellow substance.

Asher knew. It was all lost now. The defensive yellow substance from the exploding Malaysian termite, G. Sulphureus, was stronger than steel. There was nothing stopping Breitel from doing whatever he wanted now. They were so close, having destroyed most, if not all, of the other statues. Breitel had said that the energy that the statue of Asher's mother held was more than any other, and now that Asher was trapped, and so was everyone else except Simon...

Simon! Asher had to try it. He yelled up at his brother. "Simon! Wake up! Simon! Wake up! We need you!"

Nothing... Simon sat curled in the arms of his statue-mother.

Asher just wanted this all to end. He loved that he had a secret magic place, but he hated that the Painting Man, Breitel, was destroying it.

"Simon! Please! Wake up! We need you."

"He's not going to wake up," the Painting Man was saying. "He doesn't even remember who he is."

"I don't believe you. He's in there. I know he is." Asher spat these words at Breitel with deep contempt. He turned back to Simon. "Simon! Wake up! We need you now."

"I told you, he can't help you, but I can turn this all around. I can set your brother free. I can set your friends free."

"What do you mean?" Asher didn't trust him.

"My offer to you remains. Let me teach you. Let us build a stronger world together. You have abilities greater than any other I have seen. Together, we can create something better than you or I have ever seen."

"Why do you keep saying I'm so powerful? I can't stop you; obviously, if I were as powerful as you say, I would stop you right now."

"You could, you just don't know how. Only your mother, the statue right there, holds more power than you."

"Wait, you said 'your mother' as if she's still alive. Why did you say it that way?"

"No boy, she's dead. I was able to gather all of her thoughts, emotions, and energy. It's all in there, for me to use."

"If my mother's thoughts and emotions are in there…" Asher closed his eyes. He sat down on the ground. He began thinking of his mother, every detail he could remember. He thought about their time in the garden on the deck, their time at the Washington Park Zoo, their time walking through the Park Blocks studying the bugs on the trees and in the bushes. But mostly he remembered the garden and bedtime.

Bedtime was when she would hold him, stroke behind his ear, and sing to him. She would sing that nonsense song, the one he heard his father singing to Simon the other day from behind the clinic room door. He found himself singing those words now.

"Arrirang, arrirang…"

"What are you doing?" the Painting Man asked.

"Arrariyo…" and as he sang, white swirls lifted from him and flowed toward the statue.

"Stop!"

"I am crossing over Arrirang Pass."

When the white swirls from Asher's voice reached the statue, it cracked, and cracked again, and again, until white swirls burst from the cracks. The white swirls lifted Simon and gently set him on the ground.

"No! You will not stop me!" The Painting Man reached down to an exploded termite and broke off a jagged piece of the hardened yellow material. He stepped toward Asher with all his remaining strength, hand with weapon raised high, and aimed for his target. But before he could drop his hand through the branches that were the cell to the still sitting boy surrounded by white swirls, he was suddenly wrapped in web-netting.

So focused on Asher and the white swirls, he did not see that Lucie had pulled some of the web-netting free from atop the wall, climbed down and gathered it together after Mrs. Neighbors let down what was tied at the top. He could not sense her seething anger at being left on the wall, as if she were helpless. She stayed low and made her way to the Painting Man just out of his view. She swung it high and hard and held onto one side. The web-netting spread over the top of the Painting Man and interrupted his attack. She hung on and ran around him, wrapping him up, causing him to lose his balance and fall to his side, arms now pinned. He was too weak to fight against the unexpected attack; as the time passed, more and more statues were being destroyed around the Painting Man's compound. The white swirls made their way the Painting Man and twisted around him. He tried to speak but couldn't. Lucie stood over him, waiting for a reason to kick him.

The white swirls kept coming and growing. They held onto the Painting Man; they spread over the room and soon all the yellow from the termites was gone. The white swirls came to Asher's cell and the cell was… gone.

Then the exploded termite bodies were gone.

Leaf, Goldy, Pharaoh and some of the ants had made their way to the room now.

Leaf spoke, "The grubs stopped fighting. They're just crawling away."

Asher went to Simon. He sat with his little brother and held him. Simon didn't respond to the touch. Asher tried again. "Can you hear me? Are you there?"

Eyes and Legs brought, Mrs. Neighbors, and Halfwing down from the top of the wall.

Lucie moved close to Asher, stroked Simon's face, and said softly, "It's like he's one of the disconnects."

Halfwing embraced Asher and Lucie with her wings and Mrs. Neighbors laid her hands on little Simon's cheeks. Mrs. Neighbors bent further and said into Simon's ear, "Son, come back. Come back to us," but there was no response from him.

Asher suddenly turned away from Simon and toward Lucie. "Wait…what did you just say?"

"I said it's like he is one of the disconnects. I'm sorry, I didn't mean to…"

Asher jumped up and held his arms out. He started asking his mother for help. "Simon needs you, Mom. He's lost inside his mind and I can't bring him back."

The white swirls coalesced in the center of the room and spun and tightened until it took a human-shaped form, a mass of white swirls turned to white light shaped like Lynn Jakes.

Asher walked to it… to her. He stood directly in front of the glowing thing that was his mother. It was silent in the room for several moments, then… "Mom?" Asher said.

The glowing form moved closer to Asher and two wisps of light wrapped around him. He held the light form in his arms. He started sobbing, "I love you, Mom. I miss you so much, Mom. I miss you… I love you…but… Simon needs you. He needs your help."

The light of Lynn Jakes lifted out of Asher's arms and floated over to Simon. It entered Simon's body. Simon rose into the air above them all, then came back down. Simon was standing now. The light came back out of Simon and held Simon just like it had held onto Asher. Simon hugged it back and time stood still as they were one.

She raised out of Simon's embrace, floated high above them all and then shot down to the Painting Man. He convulsed in his web-made straitjacket. The light then shot out of the Painting Man and right up into the starry night.

As the light of Lynn Jakes left this world, it left a faint glow around the cocoon that held the Painting Man. As the glow dissipated, so did the walls of the compound. In a few seconds, nothing was left but open air, thousands of stars, the calling of the nearby river, and hundreds of grubs wandering aimlessly, but mostly toward the forest.

Simon turned to Asher. His chin trembled as he held out his arms and started to walk forward. "Asher? Is that you?"

Asher turned and rushed to his brother. They held each other. "I'm right here Simon. I've got you. I'm here."

Simon's face was pressed into Asher's shoulder, "Where are we? I was..."

"It's okay. I've got you now."

They pulled apart from each other for a moment. Simon looked around and saw everyone around him.

"Halfwing? Spots? Legs and Eyes! And Digger!" He was going from bug to bug, friend to friend and hugging them tightly. "I'm Simon. I... I forgot that I was Simon."

As he said the last sentence, he began to fade from Asher's view. His body was fading in and out of existence, then it twisted into a tiny speck until it was nothing.

Asher screamed out, "Simon! Simon! Where'd you go?! No! No, no, no, no...." until he felt Halfwing put her wings around him.

"Asher it's okay. He just went back to your world." Her voice calmed him.

"He did? Is that what it looks like when I go back?"

"Yes."

Mrs. Neighbors hobbled over to Asher now, dragging Lucie with her, "Come on son, it's time to go back."

"Okay." He held Mrs. Neighbor's hand and was about to pull the three of them back to the real world, but he stopped. He saw that the Painting Man, still wrapped in webbing, was no longer the Painting Man. He was now a young boy, maybe Asher's own age, or just a little older, but still unconscious.

He let go and kneeled by the Painting Man. "Halfwing! Look! The Painting Man... he..."

"I know, child. This is who he really is. This is his true form. We will take care of him, make sure he's safe and that he doesn't hurt anyone else."

Asher looked up at her, not knowing what to say. This was too much to process right now.

Mrs. Neighbors came by his side once again. "Listen son, we need to go back."

Asher stood once again and held onto Mrs. Neighbors' and Lucie's hands. He pulled them back through to the real world.

As the others watched Asher, Lucie, and Mrs. Neighbors blink out of their world, they hefted the Painting Man in the web-cocoon into the basket that Spots would carry.

Spots pulled Halfwing aside for just a moment, "Hey, Halfwing? What gives? Who's the new pipsqueak that used to be the big cheese?" He pointed to the Painting Man that was no longer the Painting Man, but a boy.

"This is who the Painting Man used to be, before he turned into the more familiar form we thought him to be. There's a chance we can save him from himself."

Spots was torn. To him, the Painting Man seemed like pure evil, but he knew to trust Halfwing.

"Let's go Spots," Halfwing said as she put a hand to his cheek. "If I'm wrong you'll be there to protect us. Of that I'm sure."

Derek Rey

Ray's Dream

ay began to wake up. He was cozy on his couch but the vividness of the dream he woke from was enough to rouse him. He dreamed of Lynn often, but this dream was so strong and clear—and different. He normally dreamed of days that he had experienced before: a walk in the Park Blocks with Lynn and the children, a day at the zoo volunteering, writing stories together at the Oregonian office, but this one was different.

Lynn visited him here in the apartment and it felt like it was now, not the past. Lynn looked different, more... alive? ...colorful? ...real? He couldn't put his thoughts together quite right.

She spoke to him and he could hear her voice as clearly as he could see the color in her bright blue eyes. She sat next to him and said, "I love you, dear. Thank you for being the father our boys need you to be. Everything is going to be fine now." Then she leaned in, kissed him as a wife kisses a husband, and held him in her arms. Ray wasn't sure exactly when it happened, but Lynn began to dissipate and float away.

Definitely the oddest and most vivid dream about Lynn he had ever had.

He laid there for several moments feeling very loved. Then the phone began to ring and grabbed his attention. "Who the heck is calling at this hour?" He stumbled his way to the phone on the counter. "Hello?"

"Mr. Jakes, it's Cody, at the OHSU satellite clinic…"

*****

Asher, Lucie, and Mrs. Neighbors all opened their eyes at the same time.

Lucie was talking before Asher could even stand. "Holy COW that was aMAZing Asher and even YOU Mrs. N.! I had no idea you were psychic like that those bugs are the best I mean they're awesome and amazing and so big and so awesome, I already said that, but still they're awesome and we were going sooooo fast on the spiders and they can jump so HIGH and Spots kind of reminds me of my dad and he's so strong like my dad and my dad told me stories of how he used to always get in fights when he was younger and Spots was good at fighting the Painting Man and it's kinda weird that Halfwing talks like Mrs. Neighbors isn't it? I mean I thought she did didn't you Asher? and it's so cool how you needed my help with the plan I feel like…" and then she punch Asher in the shoulder. "Oh yeah don't you ever put me up on a wall like that again or anything like that because I'm stronger than you and I was part of the plan and I was the one who saved you anyway and I'm serious it was soooo stupid that you told Eyes to keep me safe when everyone needed my help you're so lucky that I figured out how to get down and stop Breitel when I did because…" she stopped and just punched him in the arm again.

"I'm sorry Lucie." Asher was rubbing his definitely bruised arm as he apologized.

Mrs. Neighbors interrupted Lucie before she started up again, "Children, we need to go."

"Where?" Asher asked.

233

"Son, we need to go see Simon."

Asher's eyes shot open wide and he sat straight. "He's back?"

"Yes, son. Your father is already there."

Cody let the three of them in the locked front door, then led them back to Simon's room. Ray was talking with Simon. "Do you like your gown? Asher and Lucie put the print on it for you." Ray turned to face the others after noticing that Simon looked in their direction. Ray's wet cheeks and red eyes were the happy kind, the happiest kind. "He's awake! Asher, come and give your brother a hug."

He did.

He held his brother tightly and whispered quietly in his ear so only he could hear, "Do you remember?"

Simon whispered back, "Yes."

They held on tighter.

Asher pulled away and looked again at his brother. "You're bald."

"Whatever, you're dumb," Simon shot back without hesitation.

They both laughed, hugged each other again, and when they let go Mrs. Neighbors came forward. "I'm glad to see you back, son. Give me and Lucie each a hug and we'll let you, your brother, and your father have some time."

As Mrs. Neighbors closed the door behind her, holding Lucie's hand, she bent down and looked Lucie straight in the eye. "Listen child. I don't think you realize it, but Simon doesn't know what happened last summer. His father will have to tell him about it. He's probably doing it now. I wanted to tell you because... well remember how Asher was last summer? There were days he didn't want to play with you? Days he was just…"

"I remember. I get it, Mrs. N. I need to be careful the next time I see Simon. I will."

"But things are better now. You get that too, right?"

"Yes."

It Was a Long Time Ago

The small wooden hut was warm. Digger was curled up at the foot of the bed where the boy who used to be the Painting Man was sleeping. Digger was pressed up against the boy's feet. Spots had built a fire earlier to warm the dwelling.

Leaf was reuniting with his family. Legs and Eyes were preparing a massive feast. A raucous celebration would be taking place later that evening.

The boy moved a little and it woke Digger. He lifted his head to face the boy and saw that the boy was conscious, looking around, and he was afraid.

"Where am I?" the boy asked.

"You're… umm… here," Digger said, not meaning to be unhelpful.

"Who are you?" the boy's voice was almost in a panic.

"They call me Digger. Halfwing says that we can help you."

The boy began to calm down now, "Who is Halfwing?"

"Oh! She's nice! You'll like her. She's a moth and one of her wings is missing about two-thirds and she seems to know how to make everyone feel better when they need it."

"She's a moth?"

"Yes child, I am." Halfwing entered the room, Spots and Eyes in tow.

"You're… you're bugs!"

"Yep—we are! We might be bugs but we're tough as rocks and

ain't no one's gonna tell me different!" Spots was sparkling with confidence as he spoke.

The boy looked at Eyes and the fear came back.

Halfwing saw this and she sidled right up to the boy, laid a wing on him and said, "This is Eyes. She's friendly. She's a wonderful cook like her father. She's a wonderful builder! She built your bed."

He looked down and saw that his bed was a collection of logs of young trees, bound at each intersection with grey spider's web. The way that Halfwing spoke to him made all his fear disappear.

"Child, who are you?" Halfwing asked.

"My name is Ari. I'm alone. I ran away from home a few weeks ago."

"No, child. It wasn't a few weeks ago. It was much longer than that."

Legs peeked his head in the hut, "Food's ready! Eyes, come help your father out, I only have eight legs, I can't do it all alone."

Eyes skittered over to the boy and quickly said, "I'll show you around later, when you're feeling up to it." Then she turned and skittered out even faster.

Spots followed, "Sayonara, new kid!"

"What?" The boy was bewildered.

"Adios!"

"What?" More confusion.

"Arriva... never mind! See ya later kid!"

"Oh, yes."

Digger stayed back in the hut with the boy and Halfwing as the other bugs left for dinner. "I'm happy to watch after you, Ari. It seems you would be alone in this world if you leave this place and that would be difficult for you. For now, we're happy to be your family."

"Thank you. But Halfwing, what did you mean when you said it was 'a long time ago?'"

"Child, we will have time for that later. It's a long and confusing story, I don't even know all the parts, just mostly the ending."

The boy, Ari, looked down in resignation.

Halfwing lifted his face and stared into his eyes. "I think you'll be happy here. You have a chance to make a new life. One that makes you happy and fulfilled. I think you may have been struggling with that."

Digger spoke again, "Yes, I think so too. I'll be here to help."

"What about my father?"

"Child, I don't think you'll be seeing him again."

"Really?"

"No child, I'm so sorry."

"Don't be. He's an evil man! He wants me to be like him. He's been searching for me. If he ever catches me… he's too strong. His magic will bind me and turn me. He's been trying to make me just like him."

"You don't have to worry about him. I'm certain he's gone now."

"No! He's not! I know it!"

"Child…" Halfwing put both wings around Ari and Digger nudged up against his back, "Child, we will protect you and I'm certain he can't get you."

Ari felt a calm wash over him now. "He… he hurt my mother. My mother was trying to protect me, but she couldn't. He didn't even care that he hurt her. I'll never see her again. That's why I ran."

Digger lifted his head near to Ari's, "I'm sorry about your mother. We will do everything we can to be your family now."

Halfwing added, "Yes child, we will."

Day 5 – A Boy and His Family

"Just Take Me to the Garden"

It took all day for the doctors from OHSU to release Simon from the care facility. Simon thought it was weird how all these people knew so much about him, but he had never remembered even meeting them before, especially Cody, who treated him like a brother. Simon was like Lynn in that he knew how to receive kindness, so even though it was weird to him that Cody treated him like a brother, he knew to treat Cody with kindness in return.

Asher and Lucie spent much of the afternoon at the rocks. Lucie was peppering him with questions about the garden-world. Asher felt like he was telling her the same stories over and over, but she wanted to hear more anyway.

"Do you think we could bring Simon out here tomorrow?" Lucie asked.

"Definitely! We'll use his wagon so he doesn't have to use up too much energy. He probably would just like to hang out anyway."

It was dinner time when Simon finally made it up to the apartment with "#3" in brass above the door. He tapped the handle of the wagon on his way up the stairs (Ray was carrying him; his legs were too weak to walk up the single flight).

"Do you want to go see your bedroom? I spent all day fixing it up." Ray was excited to show Simon what he'd done. "I got you some new games. I put up some shelves to hold them all for you. I decorated the wall with sports posters and I put some glow-in-the-dark stars on the ceiling."

"Thanks Dad. No. Can you just take me to the garden for now?"

Ray understood. The garden is the closest thing he has left of his mother. "Okay, kidlet." Ray walked him out to the garden holding back and masking paternal pain. He couldn't stand that Simon was only now living the tragedy that he and Asher had been working through for an entire year.

Asher followed them out. Ray set Simon down and said, "I'm going to see if Mrs. Neighbors is ready to go down to dinner." Ray left his two boys on the deck and closed the sliding glass door behind him.

"Asher, is this where you go back and forth?"

"Yes, but we don't have time now."

"That's okay, can we go later tonight?"

"Probably, we'll see if Dad will let us stay out here."

"Can we bring Lucie?"

"Yeah, sure."

"Asher?"

"Yeah?"

"I miss Mom." He broke down again. Asher held him tightly, sitting on the deck with the garden that they built with their mother. Asher felt like he cried for two months straight last summer. At least he would be there for Simon this summer.

Dinner at J.J.'s

The entire Harper family joined the Jakeses and Mrs. Neighbors for dinner. As they stepped into the diner, Ray said, "Where's the cat? The black-and-grey tabby?"

Asher responded, "I don't think it'll be coming around anymore."

"Hmm… that's a shame, it seemed so friendly."

"I think I heard some people talking about it being lost and that it belonged to a family that was looking for it. It's probably home now." Asher and Lucie stole a knowing glance.

As K.K. seated the large party, Asher saw the newscast. Jenny Neighbors was speaking to Matthew Maxwell on a split screen.

"And when did this all happen, Matt?"

"Well Jenny, it started late last night. Each of the disconnects woke up. One after another. The ones who have been in the longest are still recovering physically, but they are all mentally one-hundred percent. The more recent disconnects have already gone home. We have a team interviewing some of them and we'll be gathering that footage into a story that we'll be airing tomorrow night."

"What does Dr. Britton say?"

"Dr. Paul Britton is here with me. Dr. Britton, what comments do you have about this wondrous turn of events?"

"Well Matt, it's too soon to share anything definitive,

but I can say with certainty that all 45 of the disconnects are healthy, either fully recovered or on their way to a full recovery. We still don't know what caused it."

"Dr. Britton, we've gotten word that Simon Jakes also happened to wake up from his coma last night. The whole city prayed for him last summer after the tragic accident, but he wasn't a disconnect. Do you know of a common thread here?"

"Well, no. We weren't counting him as a disconnect. It appeared that he was fully in a coma. We've checked him out and his father, Ray Jakes, writer for the Oregonian, has given permission for us to report on his health. We can say that he is in terrific shape. He's a bit weak right now since he hasn't exercised his muscles for the last year, but he's healthy and will be back to normal in just a few weeks."

"I bet the whole city is happy for all of this news. Thank you, Dr. Britton."

"Call me Paul."

"Well then, thank you Paul. Have a wonderful evening. Back to you in the studio, Jenny."

"Thank you, Matt. And now a startling story of corruption and mystery. A man named Anton Breitel has been buying up property here in Portland over the last year, fourteen in all. But today, when he didn't show up to a meeting with lawyers and sellers of another piece of property, the authorities were called. It appears that Mr. Breitel is missing. As police began their investigation, it became clear that Anton Breitel was not who he said he was. His documents claiming identity for his business holdings all appear to be forged. There is no record of an Anton Breitel

where he claims to be from. All of the properties sold to
Breitel will revert back to previous owners as the D.A.'s
office and court system works through this case."

Asher and Lucie looked at each other when they heard that
news. "We can stay! We can stay!!"

"Yeah, we just got off the phone with the police before we
came over to meet you," Mr. Harper said to Asher and Ray.

"Jenny told me a couple of hours ago."

"What? Why didn't you tell me, Dad?"

"I was with the doctors and Simon at the clinic and you were
with Lucie. I didn't want to leave Simon alone."

"Well, okay. I forgive you."

Ray shot him a glance. Asher looked away immediately back to
Lucie. "We get to stay!"

As J.J. and K.K. closed up the diner, Ray and the Harpers
helped clean up. The children pushed two tables together, so they
could all sit with each other. Mrs. Neighbors, Asher, and Lucie
stayed by Simon's side whispering secrets too magical for the
others to understand.

When the diner was fully closed, K.K. went into the back and
brought out a large tray filled with several milkshakes as the others
sat back down, now with J.J. and K.K. included. Everyone had
fresh blackberry from Harper's Produce. Asher and Ray added
malt. K.K. remembered that Simon only really liked vanilla, so
that's what she brought him. "Why didn't I get malt too?" he
asked.

"Because you didn't ask for it," J.J. said. "Geez Ray, teach your
kid some manners."

"Sorry, J.J. Why don't I get malt too? Please!"

J.J. snorted and took a drink of his shake through his straw. "Let me fix that for you, little buddy. Getting adventurous?"

"You have no idea!" said Simon. Asher, Lucie, and Mrs. Neighbors laughed at that response while the rest looked confused.

"Huh?"

"Uhh, nothing. Yes, I'd like malt please."

K.K. was back in a split second, seated with her own blackberry milkshake and newly added malt to Simon's vanilla.

"If you want it remade again, you're going to have to remake it yourself," J.J. said.

Simon had been treated strangely all day; he appreciated J.J.'s chiding right now; it felt comfortable and normal. "I will, sir."

Simon pulled a mouthful of malted vanilla milkshake through the straw, swallowed, furrowed his brow, paused, and said, "I don't like malt. Can you make me another vanilla shake without malt?" This time everyone laughed as K.K. got up to remake the shake, shooting a glance at her father to keep his mouth shut, with which he complied.

Ray leaned over to Simon and quietly said, only so he could hear, "You know kidlet, I like malt, and so does Asher, but your mother hated it."

"She did?"

"Yup."

They talked long into the night. Simon heard stories of the things that Asher and Lucie had done during the last year. Mr. Harper said that he still had a few cherimoyas, and that Simon could have one. Mrs. Neighbors told him that she was glad to have him back because Asher was very slow at running errands, and that he needed Simon there to stay on task and get the job done quickly.

Jenny Neighbors joined them about an hour past closing time, having finished for the evening at the news station. She sat between Ray and Mrs. Neighbors. Even with the two tables pushed together, it was a tight fit.

They all reminisced about Lynn, more happy talk. The focus seemed to be in telling the stories to Simon, instead of to everyone at the table. Normally, Simon hated being the center of attention, but this felt good.

Something was different for Ray. He felt something inside him that he didn't feel the day before. He thought, maybe... it was peace. The turmoil that had been there, right under the surface, constantly buzzing at his thoughts and emotions, ever since... well, ever since last summer... it was gone and replaced with a blanket of peace. An image stole his mind's eye. Lynn. Enrobed in light, telling him that everything would be fine now. That's when it started—the peace. It started with his dream. What a strange coincidence that that's the moment Simon woke from his come. He looked out over the table at his sons and his friends. This was his family now. He was happier in this moment than he thought he could ever possibly be again.

On the deck, Asher, Lucie, and Simon all sat by the box of Romas. There were more little yellow tomato flowers today than there were yesterday. It would be a good harvest this year.

When they made it to the garden-world, they were met by everyone at once. Spots spoke first, "Halfwing said you'd be coming and here you are! Come here, Boss!"

"I'm Simon, remember?"

"Yeah, but yer always gonna be the Boss to me!" Spots picked him up and held him high. Simon didn't really mind being called "Boss." He felt like he was Simon and he was also the Boss. He had been the Boss for nearly a year.

"Children, it's wonderful to have you back!" Halfwing was so excited to see all three under good circumstances that she even hopped and flitted her wings for a moment.

Asher spoke, "We can't stay long, my dad said we have to get to bed soon. He doesn't want Simon sleeping outside yet. My dad says his body is still healing."

"Come children—in our little bit of time, I want you to meet someone."

"Can I ride on Eyes' back?" Lucie squealed.

"Of course you can. Hop on up," Eyes said.

"You know, you have the same eyes as my friend named K.K."

"Who's that?"

"She's just a friend from our world."

Before Lucie could say any more, they were there at the hut.

They went in all together. The boy who used to be the Painting Man was sitting in the bed that Eyes had made for him. "Hello. Are you Asher? And Simon? And Lucie?"

"Yes…," they all said at once.

"I'm Ari. Thank you for saving me. Digger told me how you saved me from the Painting Man."

"But you…," Asher said but was interrupted.

"Hush child, let the boy speak."

"I'm sorry Asher, what were you going to say?"

He looked at Halfwing and looked back at the boy, Ari. He understood now; this boy, Ari, had no memory of being the

Painting Man. He indeed *was* saved from the Painting Man. "Nothing. Tell us Ari, what do you remember?"

"I was running from my father. He's an evil man. He wanted to use magic on me to make me like him, so I ran away but then I seem to have forgotten some time. Halfwing says it's been a very long time, but I don't remember any of it. I only remember waking up here and I also remember, sort of, a bright light just before I woke up. It made me feel good. It made me feel like I was safe."

Asher now knew his mother had been the one who saved Ari from the Painting Man. Her last gift. She must have sensed that Ari was inside there, needing to be saved. Asher didn't know how to say this to Ari, or even if he should. "I'm glad you're here. It's good to feel safe and Halfwing, Spots, Digger, Legs, and Eyes will take care of you."

"Digger takes care of me mostly. He acts like I wish my own father acted."

"He kind of reminds me of your dad, Asher," Lucie said.

Digger blushed at hearing this, his already dark brown skin turning two shades darker.

"We will all take care of each other," Legs spoke up now. "Asher, I promised you we'd get your brother back and promised that the Painting Man wouldn't hurt anyone anymore. We all promised." The bugs all nodded in agreement with this statement. "That promise continues still. We will be here whenever you need us."

Simon said to Ari, "These are my friends and they took care of me. I couldn't have made it without them. They'll take care of you as well."

Asher thought that a group hug with four humans and five bugs must be a sight to see. But Asher thought it was the best group hug imaginable.

Now tucked into his bed, Asher reached up for the funnel-phone.

"Lucie, you there yet?"

"Yep. Just got here. Be right back, gotta brush my teeth and put on my pajamas."

Clink

Clink

Asher's door opened. Ray walked in with Simon right behind him. "Hey kiddo, can your little brother sleep with you tonight?"

"Yeah, of course."

"I just don't want to be alone tonight. Dad and I talked for a while and I spent all day with him. I asked him if I could sleep with you tonight. Are you sure it's okay?"

"Yeah Sime, of course it's okay."

"Alright boys, I'm going to bed. Let's get up early tomorrow. Let's head up to the zoo and see some of the animals. You volunteered with Mom so much up there Simon, I bet some of the animals will recognize you."

"That's probably true," Asher said.

"Okay. Can we get breakfast at J.J.'s? His pancakes are better than yours, Dad."

Ray knew that his pancakes would never compete with J.J.'s. "No problem kidlet—J.J.'s, then the zoo."

"Can I come too?" Lucie's voice blared through the funnel-phone.

Ray grabbed Asher's end of the funnel-phone from the wall, "Yes you may. Meet us at J.J.'s at 8 a.m."

"Okay, Mr. Jakes!"

Ray gave Asher the funnel-phone and headed out, but yelled back, "Goodnight, Lucie!"

"Goodnight Mr. Jakes."

"Goodnight boys."

"Goodnight Dad," they said in unison.

Ray closed Asher's door leaving the children to themselves.

"My dad's gone," Asher said into the funnel-phone.

"Good! Can we go back and see the bugs and Ari tomorrow? I really, really, really, really want to and I want to ride on Eyes in the treetops like you got to do and I want to ride in the basket that Spots carries when he's flying and I want talk to Ari some more because he's really super old but like a kid at the same time and I want to know where he comes from and what he did back in the olden days do you think he knows he's from the olden days?…wait…to him it's only 'the days' because it was like three weeks ago to him but to us it's the olden days and that's soooooooo weird but also sooooooo cool don't you think so? and oh yeah Simon we're going to take you to the rocks tomorrow and hang out there I already decided that I'm going to bring ice cream from… I mean gelato from Bruno's and I'll make sure I bring you vanilla and doesn't that sound like a good idea?"

Simon grabbed the funnel-phone from his older brother, "You're just the way I remember you, Lucie."

"What do you mean?"

"Never mind."

Asher spoke now, "Yeah, you're right. That's pretty weird and also pretty cool. I wonder how long ago it was when he was actually a young boy, before he became the Painting Man. He told me when he was the Painting Man that he was 'hundreds of years' old. But is that three-hundred, or eight-hundred?"

Ray poked his head back in the door, "Go to sleep. I love you."

"Okay!" all three voices called back.

The door closed.

"I can't wait for tomorrow," Lucie said.

"Me either."

"Me too."

"Goodnight."

"Goodnight."

"Goodnight."

Clink

Clink

The End

Author's Notes

In the Summer of 2005, my wife, Michelle, and I took our three children (ages one, three, and five) into downtown Portland for a day of leisure. We ate at a now closed hot dog shop, grabbed coffee and hot chocolate from a local café, and we walked the length of the South Park Blocks. We were in awe of this gem of a park, right in the middle of Portland. Somewhere in the middle portion of the South Park Blocks was an art installation called "Peace Chant" by the artist Steven Gillman. My children stopped to play on and around these massive granite slabs, and in that instant, the story of Asher's Garden sprang to life in my mind. Though it took another fifteen years to write and eventually publish, the story was born, nearly fully formed, on that day.

The story and characters are completely fictitious, but I have inserted many names from my real life into this book as the names of characters. This was done in homage to important people who have weaved themselves into my own story so tightly that I couldn't imagine myself without them. They know who they are.

Thank You

To Sandy Peraza

I met Sandy in 2009. She was my coworker as we both worked in a local retail company. She stood out to me as someone with a big heart and honest desire to put goodness into the world. When I first saw Sandy's art, she was still a high school student; but even then, it was obvious that she was a talented artist with a unique eye and style. She has been featured with a multi-page spread in Thrasher Magazine, has had several commissions for board art from professional skateboarders, and has had many showings across the nation. When I was getting close to finalizing my story and researching the publishing process, I knew, without a doubt, that I wanted Sandy to do the cover art.

See more from Sandy Peraza at SandyPerazaArt.com where you could buy prints, stickers, and coffee mugs, or see her other client work, personal work, and inquire about hiring her for your art needs.

Thank You

To Tiffany Swigart

Tiffany did the lion's share of editing my book. By "lion's share," I mean to say that she found over 3000 grammar and spelling errors and, although I did not ask for story editing from her, she gave me two critical story edits that unquestionably made my story better. I am forever indebted to her for the work she did on Asher's Garden.

According to her mother, Tiffany was practically born with a book in her hand. A lover of all words, Tiffany earned a B.A. from Gonzaga University in English with a concentration in Writing. In her spare time, she is often found wrapped in a blanket with a steaming cup of tea in one hand and a book in the other. Tiffany is happy to call the beautiful Pacific Northwest home and loves exploring new places whether it's an unfamiliar country, an untrodden trail, or a lively new brewery.

I would be remiss if I did not also show my sincerest gratitude to her parents, Jill and Ron, who initially shared with me that Tiffany had the talent and discipline to edit. They were right.

Thank You

To Michelle and many others

Michelle is my wife. She consistently, but gently, encouraged me to finish this story and do whatever was necessary to get it published. Writing a first book is hard. I stumbled more than once. Michelle was there to pick me up time and time again. She had and has confidence in me and that might be the most important thing.

Thank you to my children, who inspired this story. I'd like to specifically call out my middle son who said, when I read the story out loud to him, "Dad, this is like, I think, my fifth favorite book ever! And I've read a lot of books!"

Thank you to the many readers who gave me important feedback over the years: Sam, Julie, Moira, Jennifer, Stephanie, Shannon, Mark, Crysta, Kevin, the members of the Deli Writing Group, and especially Nate, who put more effort into providing me feedback about the story and language than I ever expected; it made a real difference.

In Memory Of Don and Nola

Married in 1954.

Reunited in heaven in 2020.

Mom, Dad, this book was always for you. I love you. Thank you.

About the author

Derek Rey Pangelinan lives in the Northwest and grew up on the island of Saipan until he moved to Redmond, Oregon at the age of twelve. He is now married to Michelle and together they have three children, all boys. Outside of writing fiction, he spends time as a business/leadership coach and trainer, enjoys disc golf, loves cooking, watches too much tv and too many movies with his wife, and makes mediocre social media content.

You can find Derek at:

@DerekReyWrites on both Instagram™ and TikTok™

Discussion Guide

1. Each of the bugs in the garden-world are a reflection of someone Asher knows in his normal world. Who is a reflection of whom? What brings you to these conclusions?

2. Every parental figure does at least one important thing for their child in this story. What is an important thing that each of the following characters do for their child?
   a. Ray Jakes?
   b. Frank Harper?
   c. Anne Harper?
   d. Legs?
   e. J.J.?
   f. Lynn Jakes?

3. For whom did Mrs. Neighbors become a parental figure? How?

4. For whom did Digger become a parental figure? How?

5. In what ways is the concept of "home" a theme in Asher's Garden?

6. We learn in this story that Asher needs his friends in order to get what he wants and needs. What are some of the things

Lucie does that are so critical for Asher?

7. Asher, Lucie, and Simon prove they are capable of achieving much in this story. But we also see they are still children who are vulnerable. What are some examples of their vulnerability? Why is their vulnerability an important part of this story?

8. Arirang is a real Korean folk song. You may have to do some extra research for this, but how does the story told by the song, reflect the story of Asher's Garden?

9. Early in the book, Lucie says, "When we wake up tomorrow, I'm not going to be excited …" and at the end of the book, she says, "I can't wait for tomorrow." Discuss what it means that Lucie says these two similar, but opposite lines.

10. Asher and the Painting Man seem to have similar powers but use them differently. Specifically, they can harness human thought and emotion for their own purposes. Assume that when they use their powers, it's a metaphor. Discuss your interpretation of this metaphor.

Made in the USA
Monee, IL
11 June 2021